A MOST DANGEROUS EXCURSION!

Mildred was too shaky to even stand and stayed rooted in her seat with fear. Suddenly there was a loud *SPLOOSH!* A giant wave had broken over the lighthouse. The girls screamed and the lights flickered dangerously. Mildred's face went white. "It would definitely be a mistake to go outside right now."

"Correct!" Ms. Rapscott said jubilantly, and sat to change her boots. Lewis and Clark stood ready. "Overalls on. Steel-toed boots and rain bonnets, too, class."

The headmistress got into her raincoat and tied on her bonnet. She spun the handle on the door to the left and yanked it open. Seawater rushed in, and Ms. Rapscott squared her shoulders and splashed outside. "Remember, girls!" they heard her say, "Never be afraid to make mistakes on purpose and you will always Go Far in Life!"

OTHER BOOKS YOU MAY ENJOY

MAKING MISTAKES ON PURPOSE

MAKING MISTAKES ON PURPOSE

SEQUEL TO
MS. RAPSCOTT'S GIRLS

written and illustrated by
ELISE PRIMAVERA

PUFFIN BOOKS

PUFFIN BOOKS
An imprint of Penguin Random House LLC
375 Hudson Street
New York, New York 10014

First published in the United States of America by Dial Books for Young Readers, 2016
Published by Puffin Books, an imprint of Penguin Random House LLC, 2017

THE LIBRARY OF CONGRESS HAS CATALOGED THE DIAL BOOKS FOR YOUNG READERS EDITION AS FOLLOWS:
Names: Primavera, Elise, author.
Title: Making mistakes on purpose / Elise Primavera.
Description: New York, NY : Dial Books for Young Readers, [2016]
| Sequel to: Ms. Rapscott's girls. | Summary: "In their second term at Great Rapscott School for Girls
of Busy Parents, Ms. Rapscott teaches her students that the path to The Top starts at the Bottom of
the Barrel and other silly lessons"— Provided by publisher.
Identifiers: LCCN 2016002399 | ISBN 9780803738249 (hardcover)
Subjects: | CYAC: Teachers—Fiction. | Eccentrics and eccentricities—Fiction.
| Adventure and adventurers—Fiction. | Life skills—Fiction. | Conduct of life—Fiction.
| Boarding schools—Fiction. | Schools—Fiction.
Classification: LCC PZ7.P9354 Mak 2016 | DDC [Fic]—dc23
LC record available at https://lccn.loc.gov/2016002399

Puffin Books ISBN 9780147517685

Printed in the United States of America

10 9 8 7 6 5 4 3 2 1

Design by Jennifer Kelly
Text set in ITC Esprit Std

For Nancy Conescu, who has gone far
but will always remain a true Rapscott Girl

GREAT
RAPSCOTT
SCHOOL for GIRLS of BUSY PARENTS

Attention, Busy Parents!

You are on your way to the top . . . but is your daughter?

Statistics show that 99 percent of daughters of busy parents are in jeopardy of ending up at the bottom. Now Great Rapscott School for Girls of Busy Parents is here to do something about it!

We are proud to present our *indispensable* program designed solely for your daughter! The all NEW course:

How to Go Far in Life

Remember, busy parents, we are here to get your daughter to **The Top** where she belongs!

Classes begin promptly
on September 10th
at 7:00 a.m.*

*Be aware your daughter must be packed and ready for shipment by 6:00 a.m. (letter of instructions to follow!)

OUR MOTTO: *"Adventure is worthwhile in itself!"*
—Amelia Earhart

Dear Dr. Loulou Chissel & Dr. Lou Chissel,

We understand that you are busy. Simply follow these directions for shipping **Beatrice** to us in the convenient self-addressed box provided!

1. Place daughter, wearing school uniform, right side up in center of packing material
2. Peel off kwik-close tape
3. Fold E-Z shut flaps over top and seal*
4. Place box outside in WIDE OPEN AREA by 6:00 a.m. on September 10th
5. Leave the rest to us!

Sincerely,

Ms. Rapscott

HEADMISTRESS
GREAT RAPSCOTT SCHOOL FOR GIRLS OF BUSY PARENTS
BIG WHITE LIGHTHOUSE BY THE SEA

---

* Failure to properly seal flaps may be hazardous to your daughter's health.

Chapter 1

A Bad Start for Ms. Rapscott's Girls

On September tenth at 5:45 a.m. Beatrice Chisel pushed her box all by herself outside to a **WIDE OPEN AREA**. Bea (as she was called for short because her parents were always trying to save time) had learned a lot during the summer semester at Great Rapscott School. Formerly Known for Being Loud, Bea no longer screamed to be heard, she brushed her teeth, and she even changed her underwear daily. Bea knew that she had behaved just like a Head Girl should for the whole six-week summer break.

She hopped inside the box, settled herself comfortably into the packing material, and waited to be transported back to school. She hoped she would be Head Girl for the entire fall semester.

And why not?

Bea had pluck. Ms. Rapscott had said so the moment she saw the short sturdy girl with the choppy black hair, and Bea knew that Ms. Rapscott would be very proud of her now. But as the sky grew lighter it occurred to Bea for the first time that the box hadn't been sealed. She stood and struggled with the flaps, but the kwik-close tape was on the outside and the E-Z shut flaps were impossible to close from inside the box!

Bea gave up and flopped into the packing material to mull over the likelihood of plummeting out of an unsealed box. That's exactly what had happened to one of her classmates, Dahlia Thistle, and they'd spent the entire summer session searching for her.

To make matters worse a raindrop plopped on Bea's head. The patch of sky that she could see overhead had turned navy blue, and a gust of wind roared out of nowhere. It was strong enough to move her and the box several feet and loud enough that she never heard the large truck pull up next to her house. A moment later she felt the box being lifted.

A man grunted and said, "Wow! What's in here, rocks?"

Thank goodness! The delivery truck to take me to school . . . maybe I can ask the deliveryman to seal the box!

But it was not a delivery truck.

It was yet another one of the dangers that were constantly befalling girls of busy parents. So while it was true that Bea had learned a lot at Great Rapscott School, she still had much to learn.

That same day, around the same time, Mildred A'Lamode sat inside her own box. She'd missed the lighthouse, the corgi assistants, Lewis and Clark, and even her classmates during the break. But Mildred was Known for Being Lazy and she'd slipped back into her old ways. Ms. Rapscott was not going to be happy with her—Mildred was sure of that.

She nervously flipped through her Rapscott

journal where she'd written an account of all that had happened last semester and marveled at the many adventures she'd managed to survive. Mildred had been terrified, but she had to admit it had been exciting.

She had felt brave back then, like Amelia Earhart. In fact, they had used Amelia Earhart's very plane to fly back from one of their adventures. But since she'd been home she'd barely left her bedroom.

No, Ms. Rapscott would not approve of how Mildred had spent the break. The plump redhaired girl shifted in the packing material, aware that her uniform was too tight now. It didn't seem possible that later today she would be back at school and so far from home. What Mildred didn't know was that before the day was over she'd be on her way to a place a whole lot farther than Great Rapscott School.

On September 10th at 5:00 a.m. Annabelle Merriweather, Known for Being Old for Her Age, was ready for the fall semester at Great Rapscott

School. Her backpack was filled, she was dressed in her uniform, and the Rapscottian Medal she'd earned, "For Finding Your Way," was pinned to her sailor shirt. It gleamed from the arduous polishing she had just given it.

The box was outside in a **WIDE OPEN AREA** and all that was left to do was to get her parents to seal her inside.

Annabelle marched off to find them. She knew this part was not going to be easy.

Ms. Rapscott had said many times: "It's not that your parents don't love you, Annabelle, it's just that they're busy!" This was true, for the Merriweathers were professional exercisers and always on the go. Since she'd been at home Annabelle had tried to be more understanding and helpful. She no longer moped around reading the *Encyclopedia Britannica* all day long. Instead she put to use all that she'd learned at Great Rapscott School. She grew carrots, pruned the rosebushes, and always picked out a good cantaloupe. She knew how to do the dishes, and the laundry, and sweep crumbs off the floor. She always made sure there was plenty of toothpaste and dental floss in the house. Annabelle had learned so much at school that soon she was doing all the food shopping and even balancing her parents' checkbook.

"Good-bye," Annabelle announced as soon as she found her mother and father.

"Good-bye?" The Merriweathers stopped right in the middle of a set of push-ups—they had done 9,367 in a row and were going for a world record.

"But we're all out of peanut butter!" her father whined, and tossed her the car keys.

Ah! Peanut butter! She'd almost forgotten. Annabelle hurried into the car, and floored it. Gravel flew out from the wheels as she sped away in great haste to get her errand done and be back in time to get to school, which is how it is when you're old for your age.

At 5:55 a.m. Dahlia Thistle sat inside her box at Mt. Everbest Academy, clutching her stuffed lamb, Harold. She was very afraid. On her last trip to Great Rapscott School she'd fallen out of this very box when her parents (who held the distinction of being the two busiest people on the face of the earth) had forgotten to seal it.

"How much farther?" a voice called. Dahlia was so short that even if she stood, she couldn't see over the side of the box. She knew it was Reggie asking, though.

"Push me to a wide open area!" she shouted back.

The box stopped and Reggie's face appeared over the side. He was her favorite boy because he always seemed to know exactly how she felt. His lower lip trembled. "Are you sure you have to go?"

"I'm sure," she replied unconvincingly.

"We'll hide you if you want to stay. Right, guys?" Reggie said desperately.

Six more anxious faces were looking down at her now.

"We'll bring you food," Nathan cried.

"And we can teach you all the stuff we learn," Ernest added, and Oscar agreed.

"I can bring you crayons and paper," Theodore (who liked to draw) volunteered.

Even the new boys, twins Ricky and Nicky, were upset. "When they ask where you are—" Ricky said.

Nicky shrugged innocently. "—We'll just say we don't know!"

Dahlia shook her head. "Seal me up!"

The boys stared at her pitifully without moving.

Reggie gripped the edge of the box. "Are you sure you're sure?" he asked again.

The thing was that she wasn't sure. Dahlia reached up and placed her small hand over Reggie's. After she'd fallen out of her box she had found her way to Mt. Everbest Academy. She had worked hard to become one of the boys, and for the first time in her life she had friends. She had grown to love it there so much that now she thought of herself as an Everbest Boy. She hated to leave but if there was one thing she'd learned it was that an Everbest Boy was always brave. She squeezed her friend's hand. "Good-bye, Reggie," she whispered. Then she squared her tiny shoulders. "Seal me up!" she ordered.

Reggie's stricken face was the last thing she saw before the flaps were closed. She heard the boys call to her, "Good-bye, Dahlia! We'll miss you! Don't forget to grow!"

"Good-bye!" she called back. "I'll miss you all, too!" But her voice sounded small and far away even to herself.

Fay Mandrake woke up on September 10th at 5:45 a.m. "I'm late!" she cried. She leaped out of bed and tripped over a bucket and mop, which wasn't surprising since she slept in the broom closet.

Fay was Known for Not Being Able to Do Anything Right. Of course Ms. Rapscott saw more in the rabbity-looking girl than that—had in fact seen a definite sparkle in her eye which was a sure sign of an adventurous spirit. Fay had learned a great deal at Great Rapscott School and since she'd been home she hadn't done half as many things wrong as she used to.

That's why she couldn't believe she'd over-slept. Fay scrambled to her feet. She only had fifteen minutes to dress in her Rapscott uniform, place her box in a **WIDE OPEN AREA**, and most importantly get her little brothers and sisters to properly seal her inside. After all, she never wanted to have what had happened to Dahlia Thistle happen to her!

For weeks she had practiced over and over.

But unfortunately Fay had not gotten it right, because the flaps were not sealed promptly at 6:00 a.m. They'd been sealed at 6:01 a.m.

It was a huge mistake.

Chapter 2
A Happy Reunion

I t was a perfect day to make mistakes on purpose.
Ms. Rapscott watched through binoculars
from the lookout tower of her lighthouse that
was Great Rapscott School for Girls of Busy Parents. Clouds boiled in the sky and the wind beat
the ocean into frothy whitecaps, but that was
nothing new. Big White Lighthouse by the Sea
was located at the intersection of four storm corridors and Known for Having the Worst Weather
in the Entire World.

"Do you think there'll be a hurricane, boys?"
Ms. Rapscott asked.

Lewis poked his nose in the air and sniffed.
Clark nodded; there *would* be a hurricane.

"Thrilling!" the headmistress exclaimed.

She searched the sky again, which had turned an ominous shade of lizard green.

Ms. Rapscott peered through the binoculars and could see the first faint specks of boxes in the southern sky just over the horizon. They traveled north, one behind the other, flying directly over the cliffs straight toward the lighthouse.

"They're here!" She clattered down the spiral stairs to meet them. Lewis made sure he had his watch strapped to his wrist, and Clark grabbed his clipboard.

Outside, waves crashed against the jetty and seagulls screamed in the sky. The unrelenting wind was so fierce that the corgis had to hold on to the Great Rapscott signpost to keep from being blown away. The boxes came in at a tremendous speed, whirling around the lighthouse. Ms. Rapscott shouted, "Get ready!" The corgis scrambled into place.

Thump!

Thump!

Thump!

Thump!

The boxes landed. The corgis quickly pushed them inside, and Ms. Rapscott slammed the heavy metal door behind them with a resounding *CLANG*!

Both dogs shook off all the sand that was stuck to their fisherman's sweaters. Lewis checked his watch. It was 7:01. Clark lined the boxes up and grabbed his clipboard.

Ms. Rapscott frowned and tapped her foot. "We're missing a box."

The corgi scanned his list. He counted the boxes. He rechecked the list and recounted the boxes. He frowned as well. Then with a flick of the wrist he unzipped the E-Z open tabs.

The heads of four girls popped out of the boxes and called exuberantly, "Hello, Ms. Rapscott!"

They were all happy to see that their teacher looked exactly the same. In fact they hardly noticed anymore that Ms. Rapscott's face was the shape of a cough drop, or that her nose was far too large, or that her hair might look better in a style other than the severe bun. They were used to her nubby fisherman's sweater and the mud brown pants shoved into the no-nonsense boots. After all, those boots could slog through an alligator-infested swamp if they had to.

Lewis and Clark hardily shook Dahlia Thistle's hand first to officially welcome her as a new student. Then they went about shaking the other girls' hands as well.

Before they'd come to Great Rapscott School none of them had ever learned How to Make Friends—girls of busy parents seldom do—but now they gathered around one another excitedly, talking all at once, delighted to be back together.

"Mildred!" Bea stared at the red-haired girl. "You've gotten fat again!"

"I know." Mildred turned crimson red from embarrassment and vowed she wouldn't let this happen the next time she was shipped home. She touched Bea's school hat. It sat at a jaunty angle on the girl's head, and the ribbon that was supposed to be worn in the back hung over one ear. "You look weird with your hat that way!"

Annabelle had noticed, too. "I don't like it."

"Well, I do!" Bea said. "I think it makes me look French."

Mildred snorted. "What do you know about looking French?"

"I'm sure you're in violation of the dress code." Annabelle sniffed, but even she had to smile. Weeks of looking after her parents had made Annabelle weary. She was glad to leave the food shopping, piles of laundry, and bills behind. If anybody had ever taught her how to hug, she would have hugged Bea and Mildred right now.

"What happened to you?" Bea pointed to the large Band-Aid stuck across Annabelle's nose. But before she could answer, Dahlia Thistle, who had been largely ignored, blurted out: **"Where's Fay?"** And now for the first time the other girls noticed as well that Fay was not there!

Ms. Rapscott peered through her binoculars for what seemed like an eternity. "I see her, girls!" She grinned, showing off her two front teeth that overlapped each other and made her look like a lady buccaneer or the leader of some motley group that liked to steal from the rich and give to the poor. "Fay's made a *mistake*." Ms. Rapscott's eyes glittered. There was hardly anything she enjoyed more than mistakes because there was always so much to learn from them.

The girls gathered around their teacher anxiously. "Is Fay all right?"

"Perfectly fine!" Ms. Rapscott sounded unfazed. "I did say to be in your boxes *promptly* at six a.m., did I not, girls?"

They nodded their heads.

"A Rapscott Girl is always prompt." Ms. Rapscott waggled a finger at them and made the pronouncement, "Fay Mandrake has missed her departure time and is still at home!"

All four girls' mouths dropped open.

"Not to worry," Ms. Rapscott reassured. "Fay has made a big mistake but it will likely work to her advantage. Mistakes often do—never forget that."

She then marched to the front of the room where she stood under the clock on the wall and announced, "Take your seats, class!"

Chapter 3
ROLL CALL

There were five desks arranged in a semicircle and each girl sat at one. The middle desk was of course empty, waiting for its tardy student, Fay Mandrake. Bea, Mildred, and Annabelle glanced at Dahlia who glanced back, then all four quickly looked away without even the hint of a smile.

"When I call your name please say, 'Here.'" Then Ms. Rapscott called out the first girl's name, "Bea Chissel!"

"HERE!" Bea waved her hand. "I almost got thrown into a garbage truck!"

"A garbage truck?" Ms. Rapscott said slightly taken aback. "Now, that is truly one for the book." She nodded to Clark. "The book, please."

He reached inside the sleeve of his fisherman's

sweater and took out a medium-sized leather-bound book that was cracked with age. In it were lists of all the awful things that had happened to girls of busy parents over the years. He handed it to the headmistress, and she immediately began to thumb through it.

"Let's see now. Thrown . . . thrown . . . thrown . . . thrown from the back of a pony . . . a camel . . . an elephant . . . a pickup truck. Hmmmm . . . over the side of a rowboat . . . off the deck of an ocean liner. Ha!" She snapped the book shut and handed it back to the corgi. "Not a thing here about garbage trucks—write it down, Clark. Write it down."

Clark began to write: *Thrown into a garbage truck.*

"Wait! Wait!" Ms. Rapscott held up one hand. Clark stopped writing, his pen poised expectantly in midair.

"Bea, were you actually *thrown* into a garbage truck or were you *almost thrown*?"

"*Almost* thrown," Bea replied.

Clark added *Almost* in front of *thrown into a garbage truck.*

"Brava, Bea!" Ms. Rapscott exclaimed. "A true Rapscott Girl would *never* allow herself to be thrown into a garbage truck—unless of course she wanted to on purpose." Ms. Rapscott winked. "You haven't lost a bit of pluck over the break." Then she moved on to the next girl and called out, "Mildred A'Lamode!"

Mildred looked down. "Here?" she said in a small voice.

"You sound unsure," Ms. Rapscott observed. "A Rapscott Girl is always sure of where she is, Mildred."

Even Mildred's usually curly red hair hung limply.

Ms. Rapscott shook her head and said, "Tsk, tsk, tsk. You were doing so well before you left at the end of last semester, Mildred. What happened?"

"I don't know, Ms. Rapscott," Mildred said. But she did know—she'd done little else over the break but watch TV and eat chips.

"Your parents have been busier than ever, I assume?" Ms. Rapscott asked.

Mildred nodded. "I get to see them a lot!" Then a moment later her shoulders sagged. "But only on TV."

"Well, it can't be helped," Ms. Rapscott said with a dismissive wave of her hand. "To be a true Rapscott Girl takes time. You'll just have to do better, Mildred."

"Do you think I can?" Mildred asked.

The teacher turned to her corgis. "Can she, boys?"

Both dogs closed their eyes and nodded that she could.

Mildred felt encouraged. "I'll try harder."

"Good," Ms. Rapscott said, satisfied. Then she stepped down the line to the next girl. "Annabelle Merriweather!"

"Here," Annabelle said sharply. She tried to avoid eye contact, but of course the large Band-Aid on her nose didn't escape the teacher's notice.

"Driving again, I see, Annabelle?" Ms. Rapscott said unhappily.

"I had to do some food shopping for my parents before I left," Annabelle explained.

"You are far too young to be driving a car,"

Ms. Rapscott scolded. "You should know better, Annabelle."

"But they were all out of peanut butter," Annabelle said defensively. She looked up at the ceiling and mumbled under her breath, "It was only a fender bender."

"You must try harder to act your age, Annabelle." Ms. Rapscott sighed and turned to the last girl. "Dahlia Thistle?"

"Here!" Dahlia called out. She had blond hair cropped short like a boy's and large eyes like a baby owl.

"I've been keeping something for you." Ms. Rapscott dipped a hand inside her pocket and pulled out a bronze medal attached to a blue and silver ribbon. It was the Rapscottian Medal for Finding Your Way—the other girls had one for completing last semester's course.

Dahlia had found her way all on her own last semester and had more than proven herself worthy. "Congratulations!" Ms. Rapscott pinned it on the girl's uniform.

"Thank you, Ms. Rapscott," Dahlia said in

a tiny voice. She'd always been Known for Being a Late Bloomer, and though she'd recently bloomed, she was still far shorter than the other girls.

Dahlia was proud of herself and tried to stand a bit taller.

Bea whispered something to Mildred, then they both giggled at the new girl who had her hair slicked down and wore the sailor's tie on her uniform like a boy's.

Ms. Rapscott cleared her throat. Bea and Mildred immediately stopped their rude laughter. The teacher inquired, "Did you go home after your semester at Mt. Everbest?"

Dahlia shook her head. "My parents were too busy."

Ms. Rapscott frowned. Something was not right. Even though Dahlia had been at Mt. Everbest Academy for Boys of Busy Parents where Mr. Everbest could look after her properly, the girl had dark circles under her eyes, she had on two mismatched socks, there was a button missing on her sleeve, and that sailor tie! Lewis and

Clark discreetly retied it into a square knot for Dahlia.

Dahlia handed the headmistress an envelope.

"This is for you."

"What does it say?" Bea called out, and the others wanted to know as well.

Ms. Rapscott began to read:

Dear Ms. Rapscott,

For reasons beyond my control it appears that I have become very, very, very, very BUSY!

I am currently seeking an assistant. In fact two would be even better. Do you know of anyone who would be interested in the position?

My assistants must be able to shovel snow, do laundry, cook, fish, sled, skate, chop wood, make hot chocolate, manage unruly boys of busy parents, and most of all, forecast weather, make lists, and tell time.

I would greatly appreciate your help in this matter!

Yours truly,
Mr. Everbest

Ms. Rapscott finished the letter and looked out at her students' stunned faces. They were all thinking the same thing: What was the point of being at a school for children of busy parents if your teacher was going to be busy, too? They began to talk at the same time.

Ms. Rapscott held up a hand for quiet. "It so happens that I know the *perfect* assistants for Mr. Everbest." The teacher paused and the girls waited hopefully until she spoke. "Unfortunately . . . they are busy."

"Do you mean Lewis and Clark?" Dahlia asked.

"Of course she doesn't mean Lewis and Clark," Annabelle snapped.

"Give our corgis to those stupid boys?" Bea said incredulously.

"Never!" Mildred finished Bea's sentence.

"They're not stupid boys!" Dahlia shouted. She'd only been here a little over an hour and already she disliked this school and these girls.

The others started calling out at the same time, "They *are, too,* stupid boys!

"Girls!" Ms. Rapscott said sharply. She waited till they had simmered down, then she spoke in a calm voice. "It would never do for us to be without Lewis and Clark . . . but the two assistants that I know would be just as good."

"But Ms. Rapscott," Mildred began, "these two, who would be perfect for Mr. Everbest, they're never going to be *not* busy?"

Ms. Rapscott glanced at Lewis and Clark, who shook their heads. "No, Mildred, they're never going to be *not* busy." Then she said, "Take a letter please, Clark."

Clark clicked his pen in readiness to write. Ms. Rapscott dictated this letter:

Dear Mr. Everbest,

So sorry to hear that you have become busy. That is an unhappy turn of events!

I cannot be of help to you at this time as the only two that I know who would be qualified for the job are currently busy.

I am most sorry to add that they will never be NOT busy.

Yours sincerely,
Ms. Rapscott

Ms. Rapscott signed the letter, Clark put it in an envelope and addressed it to be mailed. Then Ms. Rapscott put Mr. Everbest's letter in her desk drawer and closed it with a *BANG!*

"What else do we have on the list, Clark?" The corgi waddled over to her and pointed to something on his clipboard.

"Oh, yes!" She inhaled deeply through her large nose and pointed a finger at the ceiling. "The seventh floor!" she intoned.

The girls waited expectantly.

"Be aware, class, that it is *off*-limits." Ms. Rapscott looked each girl in the eye. "That means *none* of you is allowed to enter that room under *any* circumstances."

Bea, Mildred, and Annabelle were somewhat startled by this new rule about the seventh floor, since they had no idea there even *was* a seventh floor.

"Any questions?" Ms. Rapscott asked. The girls gazed back at the teacher with wide, serious eyes, their heads spinning with so many questions that they didn't know which ones to ask first—so no one did. "Good," Ms. Rapscott said crisply. Then Lewis pointed to his watch and Clark checked something off his list. Both corgis nodded and Ms. Rapscott announced, "The fall semester has officially begun."

Chapter 4
HOW TO GO FAR IN LIFE

"**W**elcome to the fall semester at Great Rap-scott School for Girls of Busy Parents!" Ms. Rapscott's voice filled the round classroom.

Lewis handed out dishes of ice cream and birthday cake as he always did to make up for all the birthday parties that the girls missed because their parents were too busy.

Clark went around the room lighting the candles on their cake, and they each made a wish. "Keep your wish to yourselves, girls, or it won't come true," Ms. Rapscott reminded.

Bea wished that Ms. Rapscott would pick her to be Head Girl forever!

Mildred wished her uniform wasn't so tight.

Annabelle still thought that wishes were childish and did not believe in them.

Dahlia wished she was back at Mt. Everbest Academy.

Then Bea, Mildred, and Annabelle all sat eating their cake and ice cream, doing their best to ignore the new girl.

Bea jabbered, "I hope we go flying on the Skysweeper Winds like last semester!"

Annabelle tossed her head. "Well, I don't," she said peevishly.

Mildred didn't either. In fact, six weeks at home had made her feel utterly hopeless and out of practice for such things. She couldn't help admiring Bea who made everything look so easy. "I wish I was more like you, Bea." She sighed.

"You do?" Bea said it as if she was surprised, but she really wasn't. Who wouldn't want to be like her: always first, fast, and full of pluck! Still, even though Mildred was always last and had trouble keeping up, Bea secretly liked her the best. Mildred was never cross like Annabelle and never tried to butt in front of her like Fay. "But you're nice, Mildred," Bea whispered.

"Big deal," Mildred said glumly.

Dahlia longingly stole a look at her new classmates who talked among themselves so easily and freely—just the way she used to talk with the boys at Mt. Everbest. She patted the pocket on her jacket where she'd placed Harold. Mr. Everbest had been so busy lately that he'd forgotten and put the stuffed lamb in the dryer and shrunk him to half his size. Now Harold fit into the smallest places, and Dahlia took comfort in knowing he was there.

"Delicious!" Ms. Rapscott finished her cake. It was cherry with chocolate chips, vanilla filling, and chocolate icing—and better than ever.

Lewis collected all the dishes and was back in a flash. The girls couldn't help but notice that he was checking his watch. The color drained from Mildred's face because it was almost 9:00 a.m., and she knew from past experience that the course was about to begin.

Next Clark entered the classroom with several

full backpacks which could only mean one thing: Soon the girls would be on their way to somewhere unlike any place they could ever imagine.

"May I have your attention, please!" Ms. Rapscott exclaimed.

The girls hardly dared to draw a breath.

Ms. Rapscott clasped her hands in front of her. All that could be heard was the *ticktock, ticktock* of the clock on the wall. "This semester you will be taking an *even more* difficult course than last." She smiled broadly as if she was proposing an afternoon at the circus filled with cotton candy and peanuts. Ms. Rapscott loved it when things became *more* difficult. "This semester's course will be: HOW TO GO FAR IN LIFE."

Clark placed a backpack next to each girl, and they wasted no time in going through them to look for clues as to what was in store for them.

Here is what the girls found:

Official Rapscott raincoat
Boots
Rain bonnet

Mug

Spoon

Hot chocolate

Overalls

Steel-toed boots

Blanket

Birthday balloons

Slippers

Pillow

Hard hat with light

Mildred was speechless with dread. She did not like being outside and she liked it even less if it involved a hard hat and steel-toed boots.

Clark tapped his pointer on the chalkboard for quiet, and Ms. Rapscott spoke again.

"You will be graded on the following: grit, kindness, patience, and bravery."

Bea shouted out, "What if we fail?"

"You will undoubtedly fail," the headmistress said delightedly, and there was an audible gasp from the girls.

Annabelle bristled at this latest outrage. Getting lost on purpose was one thing, but what kind of a school encouraged failing?

"You cannot Go Far in Life unless you fail several times," Ms. Rapscott replied with a wave of her hand. "Any more questions?"

"But Ms. Rapscott, how will we know we passed, then?" Bea asked.

"You cannot pass the course until you've reached The Top, and you cannot reach The Top unless you Go Far." Ms. Rapscott snapped her fingers. "You will know you passed when you earn the Great Rapscott Medal for Reaching The Top!" She pointed to the closet. Clark trotted over to it and came back with a case. Inside, five gold medals were attached like pendants to blue and silver ribbons that could be worn around the neck. Inside the pendant was the etching of the lighthouse, and a diamond shone in the center of the light. Clark went to each girl so that she could get a good look. It was the most beautiful medal that any of them had ever seen, and they all wanted one, especially Bea.

"What's grit?" Bea asked.

Lewis instantly handed Ms. Rapscott the dictionary. "Let's see . . . grim . . . grime . . . gristle . . ."

"Grit!" Dahlia Thistle called out. All heads turned to stare at the new girl as she stood and recited, "Firmness of mind or spirit; unyielding courage in the face of hardship or danger. Grit!"

"Very *good* Dahlia," Ms. Rapscott said, impressed.

"Show-off," Bea muttered. Mildred and Annabelle could not have been less impressed.

But Dahlia wasn't being a show-off at all. She had heard the word from her teacher, Mr. Everbest, who had told her she had "grit" and lots of it. At first Dahlia hadn't believed him because she couldn't even get down the mountain in a toboggan without covering her eyes. But she always brought Harold with her, and the more adventures she went on with the boys at Mt. Everbest the braver she'd become. She'd worn the same blazer and khaki pants as the boys, and even had her hair cut like them. By the end of the term she had turned into an Everbest Boy.

But she wasn't at Mt. Everbest anymore—she was at Great Rapscott and expected to be a Rapscott Girl now.

The clock struck 9:00 and Lewis nodded.

"The course has begun!" Ms. Rapscott announced. "Question Number One! In order to get to The Top one must start where?"

The girls looked at one another to see if anyone knew, but none of them did.

"The Bottom, class!" Ms. Rapscott paced back and forth in front of the girls as she spoke and held a finger in the air. "The Bottom; a cold place made of solid rock, with unpleasant rules. A place where no one listens to you and where even if you think you're ahead you're actually behind."

"But that's not fair!" Annabelle called out.

Ms. Rapscott widened her eyes and said, "Precisely!"

"I don't want to go to The Bottom," Mildred cried.

"I do!" Bea said confidently. "Yay! When do we leave?"

Annabelle rolled her eyes.

Dahlia had made up her mind there was no adventure any scarier then being right here in this room with these girls. She was anxious to get started, too.

Mildred was not. "But how are we expected to manage in such an awful place?" she asked.

"You will have to rise above it, Mildred. **Question Number Two!**" Ms. Rapscott announced. "How do we get to The Bottom?"

Once again none of the girls knew.

"Come, come, girls," Ms. Rapscott said. "Doesn't anyone even want to take a guess?"

The girls all shook their heads.

Ms. Rapscott was surprised. "Why not?"

Bea spoke. "Because we might make a mistake."

"Correct!" Ms. Rapscott said, and she made a little hop for joy. "*Mistakes*, girls!" she exclaimed. "We must Make Mistakes on Purpose to get to The Bottom!"

Annabelle did not like lessons about failure and mistakes and sighed loudly to show that she disapproved.

The headmistress took the pair of overalls that Lewis handed her. The corgis were already dressed in theirs. She shoved one leg into the baggy pants, then the other. She pulled up the zipper with a loud *Z-I-I-I-I-P*! Then she closed one eye and cocked her head as if she was listening intently for something. "The water has risen," she whispered. "Can you hear it?"

They all listened and could hear a faint gurgling sound.

Ms. Rapscott stood still to hear until she was very sure. "It's the Grim Tidings, girls," she said in a deep voice.

The girls sat motionless listening to the alarming sound of a great amount of water sloshing around like a gigantic washing machine.

"Mildred, do you think it would be wise to go outside right now?" Ms. Rapscott asked.

Mildred was too shaky to even stand and stayed rooted in her seat with fear. Suddenly there was a loud *SPLOOSH!* A giant wave had broken over the lighthouse. The girls screamed and the lights flickered dangerously. Mildred's face went white. "It would definitely be a mistake to go outside right now."

"Correct!" Ms. Rapscott said jubilantly, and sat to change her boots. Lewis and Clark stood ready. "Overalls on. Steel-toed boots and rain bonnets, too, class."

The headmistress got into her raincoat and tied on her bonnet. She spun the handle on the door to the left and yanked it open. Seawater rushed in, and Ms. Rapscott squared her shoulders and splashed outside. "Remember, girls!" they heard her say, "Never be afraid to make mistakes on purpose and you will always Go Far in Life!"

Chapter 5
THE BOTTOM BY WAY OF BARREL

Bea Chissel made sure she was the first one to poke her head outside the school door and was shocked to see that the jetty with the pointy rocks, the sand with the sea grass, and the land that connected them to the island were covered entirely in water.

The classroom was soon flooded, and the others sloshed as quickly behind as they could.

"We're in the middle of the ocean!" Mildred pressed her back against the lighthouse wall while seawater covered her steel-toed boots. "Where did the land go?"

"It's the Grim Tidings!" Ms. Rapscott's eyes

glittered with excitement. "Every year right around this time we are given a warning, girls."

"What kind of a warning?" Mildred did not like the sound of that.

"A *grim* warning, Mildred." Ms. Rapscott explained, "First we get extremely high tides called the Grim Tidings, followed by an enormous wave, warning us that hurricane season will begin any minute."

"Hurricane season! Yay!" Bea called out.

Annabelle gave Bea a dirty look. "Surely, Ms. Rapscott, you can't mean that we're going to be out in a hurricane today?"

Clark nodded and pulled a small well-worn book from his sleeve, thumbed through it, then handed it to the teacher opened to a certain page. Ms. Rapscott's eyes lit up. "Today we will be having Hurricane Bertha and for the remainder of the semester we will be visited by Hurricane Bessie, Birdie, Bobby, Brunhilda, Bunny, and Buster to name a few—and every single one of them is known for being a ferocious storm in their own way."

The water inched higher up Annabelle's shins and her voice rose with it. "But, Ms. Rapscott, don't you think that we should heed the warning of the Grim Tidings and go back inside?"

"Would it be a mistake not to, Annabelle?" Ms. Rapscott asked.

"Of course it would be a mistake," Annabelle barked.

"Then we *must* stay outside—otherwise we'll never get to The Bottom," Ms. Rapscott insisted. There was a rumbling sound from over the horizon. "Look, girls, here comes the enormous wave, and it's right on time!"

Sure enough, just over the horizon, headed right toward them was a wave that appeared to be frightfully larger than a wave should be. Mildred wrung her hands and tried to remember what it was about the Great Rapscott School that she had come to love by the end of last semester, but at the moment she couldn't come up with a thing.

All but Bea watched with horror as the water from the Grim Tidings rose to their knees. They clung to the posts on the porch in the hopes that they wouldn't be yanked out to sea when the wave crashed down upon them. Suddenly a large oak barrel floated from around the side of the lighthouse. The lid came off and out popped a rotund man with a mustache, wearing a top hat and an important-looking sash across his chest. "What ho, Ms. Rapscott!" he called out, and paddled closer.

"Well, well, well, if it isn't our mayor!" Ms. Rapscott replied. "Say hello, girls—a Rapscott Girl is always polite."

The girls mumbled hello, their eyes riveted on the ominous wave speeding ever closer.

"Making mistakes on purpose, I see?" Ms. Rapscott shouted to the mayor.

"Yes! It's the most successful way to fail, don't you think Ms. Rapscott?" he shouted back.

"Especially if you want to go far!" she called to him.

The wave tumbled nearer by the second, and the wind whirled around the lighthouse in a most nerve-jangling way. "What are we going to do, Ms. Rapscott?" Mildred asked anxiously.

Ms. Rapscott seemed in no hurry. "Hmmmm."

She straightened her bonnet and calmly listed their options. "We could go back inside the lighthouse and learn How to Peel a Hard-boiled Egg—which I'm sure your parents were always too busy to teach you." She called out to the mayor again. "Or perhaps our mayor would be so good as to let us borrow his barrel?"

The mayor paddled up to the lighthouse and climbed out of the large barrel that could easily fit four girls, two corgis, and a teacher. He tipped his top hat. "Mind you, Ms. Rapscott, this is entirely against my better judgment."

"It's a terrible idea," she agreed merrily.

"Me! Me!!" Bea shouted, and jumped up and down, eager to be put in the barrel first.

Clark scooped her up, Lewis lifted Mildred, and the mayor held the barrel while Ms. Rapscott put Dahlia inside. Lastly Lewis and Clark grabbed Annabelle under her arms and swung her in there as well.

"This is not right," Annabelle sputtered.

"It's a huge mistake, all right," Dahlia said, glad that she'd brought Harold along with her.

"But there's no better way than by barrel to get to The Bottom, don't you agree?" Ms. Rapscott asked the mayor.

"Oh, yes, Ms. Rapscott," he heartily agreed.

"Off we go, then!" Ms. Rapscott exclaimed. She climbed in, followed by the corgis who used the paddle to push them from the lighthouse porch just as the enormous wave came rushing in.

WHOOOOSH! An extraordinarily strong gust of wind blew the mayor away. He circled the top of the lighthouse once. "Good-bye!" he called. "I hope you go far!"

"I hope you do, too!" Ms. Rapscott shouted back.

The wave caught the barrel with tremendous force, and they surged forward, bobbing along in the bubbly foam toward the shore. Then just as suddenly the wave retracted and they were pulled back the other way. The girls peeked over the rim and watched helplessly as they were dragged out to sea. The light from the Great Rapscott School blinked dimmer and dimmer until it was gone entirely.

They passed many boats caught in the tidings, too. Bea remembered her lessons well from the summer session and waved at the people on the fishing and lobster boats.

Ms. Rapscott approved. "A Rapscott Girl is always friendly."

Annabelle sulked, refusing to wave back, and Mildred was too sick to her stomach to do anything more than cling to the side of the barrel and try not to throw up.

The farther they went the fewer people they saw. The barrel sailed up one side of tall waves and careened down the other. They finally passed a lone cruise ship and soon even that was just a speck in the distance.

"This is even more of a mistake than I thought it would be." Ms. Rapscott laughed and leaned over the edge of the barrel to feel the spray from the briny sea on her face. "Isn't it thrilling!" she exclaimed.

"Thrilling!" Bea agreed. She was not the least bit afraid and wondered what Ms. Rapscott had meant about this semester being so difficult? So far it was easy.

Dahlia, too, was not exactly enjoying herself, but thought it no worse than last semester when she'd had to find her way all by herself. It was definitely better than being in her box, sure that she was going to tumble out any second, or listening to these awful girls call the boys at Mt. Everbest stupid.

Mildred's stomach lurched as they raced up and down the sides of waves as tall as mountains, and she wondered how this could possibly be good for her.

"I think I'm going to throw up," Mildred said.

"Not now, Mildred." Ms. Rapscott looked through her binoculars. "We've got Bertha off the starboard side!" Sure enough, winds swirled eerily in the distance and arranged themselves into a shape. The sky was soon filled with the enormous face of a woman made out of clouds. "It would be a terrible mistake to head straight for her!"

Lewis and Clark immediately set to paddling in that direction, but they needn't have tried too hard because Bertha took a deep breath. The barrel was sucked right into the middle of the hurricane just as Bertha began to blow. Her cheeks filled with air until they looked like they might explode, and her breath hit the barrel broadside as if it'd been shot out of a cannon. The girls could do nothing but hold on for dear life. They flew across the ocean, rain pelting them with such force that not even the Rapscott raincoats and bonnets could keep them dry now.

Ms. Rapscott was very happy with the way things had gone so far and shouted, "If we keep on making mistakes like this we should be at The Bottom in no time, class!"

Chapter 6
THE BOTTOM

Clark pulled the lid down over the barrel, and they were plunged into darkness. They sat stuffed in the barrel, in the middle of the ocean with waves crashing down all around. Waiting to be sunk or smashed into bits even made Bea start to worry. She reached for Mildred's hand. Mildred in turn grabbed Annabelle's and Annabelle was about to take Dahlia's when something stopped her.

What if Dahlia Thistle's hand is squishy and damp, or slimy, or cold as ice? What if her hand grips mine too hard? What if Dahlia Thistle has never learned to wash her hands after using the bathroom . . . heaven only knows what those revolting boys were being taught at that awful Mt.

Everbest Academy. They probably have never even heard that you're not supposed to put your fingers in your nose!

Annabelle withdrew her hand like she'd just touched a hot griddle—no way was she going to hold a hand she knew nothing about.

Even though Dahlia knew she had a lot of grit, she still longed for someone to hold her hand. But no one would. More than ever she missed her friends at Mt. Everbest—particularly Reggie who'd held her hand more than once on many hair-raising toboggan rides down Mt. Everbest. Her only friend now was Harold. She took hold of the stuffed lamb's tiny cloven hoof.

For some time Ms. Rapscott's four girls stayed squashed together inside the barrel, being tossed about from wave to wave. Just as Bea was beginning to wonder if all these mistakes were such a great idea, the barrel was hurled into the air by a particularly violent wave. The barrel hovered, dropped, and smacked the water hard, then plunged beneath the sea.

Down,

    down,

        down, the barrel went.

"We're sinking!" Annabelle shrieked.

"Correct, Annabelle!" Ms. Rapscott shouted back. "Hold on, girls!"

GLUG . . .

    GLUG . . .

        GLUG.

            The barrel plunged.

Bea, Mildred, Annabelle, and Dahlia braced themselves for what was to come next.

CRASH! The barrel landed on what should have been the ocean floor, and the girl's teeth rattled inside their heads, but The Bottom was farther still!

BUMP!

    BUMP!

        BUMPETY!

            BUMP!

                BUMP!

They bounced down what seemed like a long flight of stairs. Then it rolled once . . . twice . . . three times and came to a complete stop.

All was silent.

Lewis checked his watch, and Clark made a note: 12:17 p.m. Then he cautiously popped off the lid, relieved to see that they were on dry ground. Bea was first and the other girls crawled out after her.

Bea, Mildred, and Annabelle leaned on one another to stand (leaving Dahlia to pick herself up). They each tried to get their bearings in the dimly lit room with the gray floor and gray walls lined with gray chairs.

"Raincoats off!" Ms. Rapscott ordered. "Bonnets, too, class!"

Lewis and Clark tested the ground by jumping up and down a few times. They put their ears to a wall, alternately knocking with their paws, listening for some sound until, satisfied, they nodded to Ms. Rapscott.

"Solid rock, class," she proclaimed. "Congratulations! You've *officially* reached The Bottom!"

As if on cue a glass window, where there was none before, slid open. Behind the window a receptionist was seated. She was a little round woman dressed in a gold sparkly uniform, and on the tip of her nose was a mole in the shape of a star. On her head was a tall pointy gold hat, and when she leaned forward half of it stuck out into the room. "If it isn't Ms. Rapscott!" she exclaimed. "Trying to get to The Top, I assume?"

"Correct!" Ms. Rapscott answered.

"Take a number." The little woman pointed the end of her hat at a dispenser on the other side of the room.

Annabelle pulled one from it. "One million, six hundred thousand, three hundred eighty-nine?" she said with much indignation since they were the only ones in the awful all gray, solid rock room.

The receptionist was having a snack and intently placed a cube of cheese on a cracker. She never looked up and in a singsong voice said, "Indignation is frowned upon at The Bottom."

Ms. Rapscott quickly intervened. "I'm afraid this is the girls' first time at The Bottom, and they don't know the rules."

The little woman put down her cracker and cheese and recited, "The rules: no indignation, no sighing, and no stuffed animals." She went back to her cube of cheese, which she carefully balanced on the cracker. Just as she was about to pop it in her mouth, she stopped. Her nosed twitched. She sniffed the air and said, "I smell a stuffed animal."

Dahlia stood frozen in place. Her heart hopscotched around in her chest. The hand that held Harold's hoof trembled, and she could swear she felt him shiver with fear. She gripped the stuffed lamb even tighter.

The other girls watched with wide eyes.

The receptionist brushed cracker crumbs off her desk and spoke through pursed lips, "I *said*, no stuffed animals."

Dahlia tried not to cry but it wasn't easy. "This is the worst thing that could ever happen."

"Brava, Dahlia!" Ms. Rapscott exclaimed, and made a little hop for joy. "It's always such a wonderful relief to have the worst thing happen—isn't that right, boys?" Lewis and Clark nodded that it was right.

Dahlia felt anything but relieved. She took Harold out of her pocket. She kissed his nose, and he looked at her with pleading eyes. The receptionist reached out her pudgy hand that still had cracker crumbs stuck to it and plucked him from her.

"Take a seat." She snapped the glass window shut.

"I always say," Ms. Rapscott continued as she settled herself into a rock hard chair, "it's good to have the worst thing happen because then things can only get better!" Clark seemed to like this because he instantly wrote it down to use for some future Remark of the Day. Ms. Rapscott hummed, quite pleased, as she waited. The corgis swung their legs which were too short to reach the ground.

Bea sat down hard and scowled at the number in her hand. She was anxious to get out of the horrid room and away from this awful receptionist.

Mildred twirled her hair nervously.

Annabelle sighed.

The glass window flew open again. "No sighing." The receptionist just as quickly slid the window shut again.

Bea marched up and banged on the window. "Hey!" She pressed her nose against the glass. "How long are we supposed to wait?"

The receptionist never looked up. She remained engrossed in setting up a row of crackers where she placed a cube of cheese on each and ignored Bea as if she weren't even there. "Hello?" Bea banged again on the window. "I'm talking to you!"

"You might just as well save your breath, Bea," Ms. Rapscott said with resignation. "No one wants to listen to you when you're at The Bottom."

"But that's not fair!" Bea cried.

"Precisely!" Ms. Rapscott said.

The four girls waited in this miserable fashion for some minutes when all of a sudden the dreadful silence was broken by a distant *bumpety, bump, bumping* sound. It became louder and seemed to come from the very stairs they had just rolled down in their barrel only minutes before.

BUMP!

   BUMP!

      BUMPETY!

         BUMP!

            BUMP!

"Watch your toes, class!" Ms. Rapscott drew up her feet just as another large barrel bounced into the room, rolled, ricocheted off the opposite wall, and came to a complete stop beside their own. The top popped off and out tumbled seven boys and a man.

"Why if it isn't Mr. Everbest!" Ms. Rapscott said, pleasantly surprised.

"Ms. Rapscott!" He was equally delighted to see the headmistress once again.

"Reggie!" Dahlia ran to the boy as he scrambled to his feet. She was so happy to see her friend that she threw her arms around him even though she'd never been taught How to Hug.

"Oh, I knew this would happen!" Reggie moaned. The other boys crowded around her, just as concerned. At school they were always reminding Dahlia to grow—which is how it is when you're Known for Being a Late Bloomer. "You've already gotten smaller!" they all said.

Dahlia averted her eyes, "No I haven't."

"Yes, you have!" Reggie cried. "You've shrunk a bit just since this morning!"

"That's ridiculous," Dahlia replied but, in actual fact, she did feel a smidge smaller.

The new boys Ricky and Nicky immediately knew what was wrong. After all, when the other Everbest Boys weren't hiding the twins' mittens they were stealing their birthday cake. Ricky whispered in her ear, "Are they being mean to you because you're new?"

"No, I'm fine, I really am," Dahlia said, though she wasn't at all.

Then Oscar, who secretly wished he owned a stuffed animal even though he knew he was too old for one, asked, "How's Harold?"

"Gone!" Dahlia cried.

"Gone?" The boys said as a group in disbelief because they knew Dahlia never went anywhere without Harold.

"It's the worst that could happen!" Dahlia moaned. "Stuffed animals aren't allowed at The Bottom."

The boys were outraged, but Annabelle was tired of all this fuss over a stupid toy lamb. She rolled her eyes and exclaimed, "For heaven's sake it's not like he's *real*!"

Reggie's face darkened. "Why don't you ditch this group and come with us?" He pointed over his shoulder with his thumb at the girls.

Dahlia wished she could, but she had grit! She would never let those Rapscott Girls know that they were bothering her. "Shhh." Dahlia held a finger to her lips.

But Bea had already heard and stuck her tongue out at Reggie.

So Reggie stuck his tongue out at Bea.

"No, Reggie!" Dahlia cried, because she knew it would only make things worse. But it was too late. The other boys marched over to Bea, Mildred, and Annabelle.

"You'd better be nice to our friend Dahlia!" Ricky and Nicky held up their fists like they were ready to fight. Dahlia had to smile. The twins were always fighting with each other, but here they were coming to her defense!

Ernest made a rude noise, Theodore made a

horrible face, Ricky called Mildred, "Mildew," Nicky called Bea, "Pee." Finally Nathan crowed, "I bet we beat you dopey girls to The Top!"

"I bet you don't!" Bea held up her fists, ready to knock the boy's block off, but Annabelle held her back.

"Pay no attention to them," Mr. Everbest called jovially to the girls. "They're really good boys—they're just Doing Their Best at Being Their Worst!"

Ms. Rapscott's eyes lit up. "Why, I never thought of that. What a marvelous way to get to The Bottom."

"However did *you* get here?" Mr. Everbest inquired.

"Mistakes, Mr. Everbest," Ms. Rapscott replied conspiratorially. "We've made many, *many* mistakes— but it's a marvelous way to Go Far in Life."

Mr. Everbest nodded in approval and whispered, "It's my ninety-ninth try, Ms. Rapscott, and *this* time I'm going all the way to The Top if it's the last thing I do."

"But Mr. Everbest, you seem to be missing a boot." Ms. Rapscott couldn't help noticing.

He looked down and laughed at himself. "Ah! So I am! I'm in a big hurry—been busy, you know—and while we're on the subject, thank you for your speedy response to my letter—took on two new boys—the twins here, Ricky and Nicky." They were small wiry boys with curly dark hair who stood shyly off to one side apart from the others.

Ms. Rapscott and Mr. Everbest watched as the one boy said something to the other. The other said something back and poked his brother. Then Ricky poked his brother back, and Nicky slapped Ricky, and in a split second they were both rolling around on the floor in a tangle of arms and legs calling each other horrible names.

"They're a handful," Mr. Everbest confided, "and Known for Calling Each Other Horrible Names. I didn't want to take them on but in all good conscience I had to."

"Why is that?" Ms. Rapscott inquired.

"RATFINK!" Nicky yelled, and twisted Ricky's arm.

"FERRET FACE," Ricky yelled back, and held a hank of Nicky's hair tightly in his fist, doing his best to pull it out by the roots.

Mr. Everbest shook his head. "Their parents are both running for office—very busy pair they are! But the boys barely know the difference between a snowball and a basketball."

"Tsk, tsk," Ms. Rapscott said sympathetically.

Ricky had Nicky in a headlock. "LYING LOUT!" Ricky yelled.

"GREAT GIT!" Nicky retaliated in a strangled cry.

"See what I mean?" Mr. Everbest said.

"I do!" Ms. Rapscott replied.

The headmaster reached into his pocket and pulled out Ms. Rapscott's letter. "But is it really *true*? The two assistants you speak of—will they never be *not* busy?"

Ms. Rapscott turned to Lewis and Clark. "Boys?"

The corgis nodded sadly.

"I'm afraid it's all too true, Mr. Everbest," Ms. Rapscott said.

Suddenly the glass window slid open, and the receptionist leaned out. "Take a number," she ordered the boys just as she had the girls. Oscar ripped off the ticket, and the others crowded around to see.

"Number three!" the receptionist called.

"That's us!" Oscar shouted.

"But it *can't* be," Bea said bewildered. "We were here *first*."

A door opened and the boys scurried out of it. "Mr. Everbest!" Ms. Rapscott dipped into her backpack and pulled out a large boot. "I have a spare!"

"Thanks!" Mr. Everbest shouted back. "But no time—gotta run!"

Bea wailed, "We were here first!" She stamped her foot. "It's not FAIR!!!!"

"Nothing ever is at The Bottom," Ms. Rapscott said. "But we must make the best of a bad situation, class." She hurried through the door that remained open for only a few seconds. Thrilled to be sneaking out, Bea got right in behind Ms. Rapscott and scurried to the other side. Mildred went next, her heart in her throat, certain that the door would slam shut on her.

"I'm sure this is not allowed," Annabelle said. But she was not about to get left behind. She zipped through the door, glad to be out of the awful solid rock room with the little bossy woman in the gold uniform.

Dahlia Thistle looked wistfully over her shoulder. She reached into the pocket where her stuffed lamb always was, and it felt shockingly empty as if she'd lost a part of herself . . . as if she'd just touched her head only to find all her hair missing. How could she leave without Harold?

"Harold!" she called. But of course no one heard her, which is how it is when you are at The Bottom. She slipped reluctantly through the door right before it clamped shut behind her.

"Come along, girls," Ms. Rapscott said. "We have nowhere to go but up!"

Chapter 7
THINGS GET WORSE ON PURPOSE

Mr. Everbest and his boys had run ahead, and Ricky and Nicky's horrible name calling grew fainter by the second. Lewis checked his watch: 1:00 p.m. on the dot. Clark wrote it down. The girls huddled together. On the one hand they were glad to be rid of the gloomy gray room, but it was even gloomier here.

"Hard hats on, class!" Ms. Rapscott ordered. Lewis and Clark helped the girls with the buckles that snapped under their chins. A small beam of light appeared and Ms. Rapscott pointed to a little red button on the side of her hat. "Push this."

Mildred pushed hers and, to her dismay,

wherever she pointed the light she saw bats circling overhead, water dripping from the ceiling, and lumps of coal at her feet. "We're no better off here than we were before," Mildred groaned.

"Correct, Mildred!" Ms. Rapscott said. "But in order for us to rise above The Bottom we need to be *much* worse off!"

"But Ms. Rapscott . . ." Mildred's voice was almost a whimper, "we're in a coal mine."

"And it's past lunch and I'm starving," Bea added.

"And I'm cold and my feet are wet," Annabelle complained.

"And I've lost Harold," Dahlia cried. "How could we be any worse off?"

"Hmmmm, how could we be any worse off . . . how . . . how?" Ms. Rapscott tapped her chin with a finger. She tilted her head, squinted, and considered her red-haired student. "Perhaps Mildred could help."

Mildred's mouth instantly went dry.

Ms. Rapscott was pensive. "I'm wondering,

Mildred . . ." the headmistress folded her arms, closed one eye, and studied Mildred with the other, "if you were to lead us to the exit do you think you might hold us up terribly?"

"I-I'm sure I would." Mildred looked down and shook her head. She wrung her hands at the very thought of it. "I'm such a slowpoke."

Ms. Rapscott brightened. "In that case it would probably take *days* to get to find the exit— or maybe even *months*."

"Months?" All four girls exchanged worried looks.

"Yes, yes. Mildred will lead us!" Ms. Rapscott was very pleased with her idea for it would definitely make things worse.

"Oh, please don't make me lead," Mildred pleaded. "I'll be awful at it!"

Bea raised her hand. "I'll be a good leader, Ms. Rapscott. Pick me!"

Ms. Rapscott shook her head. "Oh, no, that wouldn't do at all, Bea. It would be *much* worse for you if you went last."

"But I hate to be last," Bea cried.

"Precisely, Bea. And that will make things worse for everyone," Ms. Rapscott said. "But things could be even *worse*."

"No!" All four girls chimed in at once. "How could things be worse, Ms. Rapscott? How?"

"For instance." Ms. Rapscott knew exactly how. "Say I had Harold—"

"You have Harold?" Dahlia said hopefully.

Ms. Rapscott instantly inexplicably produced the stuffed lamb from her pocket. "And say, I gave him to Annabelle to carry, she would probably be worse off than she is now."

"Of course I would!" Annabelle gave Dahlia a scornful look, remembering that she'd just sided with those revolting boys. "Only babies carry such things."

"Harold!" Dahlia reached for him with both hands as Ms. Rapscott passed over the tiny girl and handed him to Annabelle.

"Harold?" Annabelle cringed and held him by his tail, certain that he was probably crawling with germs.

The four stood in various states of unhappiness, far worse off than they had been before.

Mildred was full of dread at having to lead.

Bea was crushed to have to be last and walk behind everyone else.

Dahlia was bereft without Harold, and Annabelle wanted to fling him as far as she could.

Ms. Rapscott was delighted beyond words. "Congratulations, girls! I am happy to inform you that things are *officially* at their worst!"

Ms. Rapscott pointed with great fervor down the dark creepy path that descended even deeper into the earth. "Off we go! We must find the exit!" All the girls could see was a tunnel with a narrow rocky trail and more bats. "Lead us, Mildred!"

Mildred shuddered, but of course she knew there was no choice but to do as she was told and lead them to the exit, wherever that was. She took a few hesitant steps to pick her way over rocks and coal. Already the straps from her backpack dug into her shoulders, and her stomach rumbled with hunger.

"Hurry *up*!" Bea yelled impatiently from the end of the line.

Mildred could feel her classmates' eyes boring a hole in her back. They grew angrier by the minute, wanting her to go faster, but the way was steep and she stumbled often. The deeper into the mine she led them the hotter it became. The air was stale, cobwebs stuck to her sweaty face, and her legs felt heavy. The worst of it, though, was knowing how much she was holding everybody up and that even Bea was mad at her now. "Oh, how much farther is the exit?" Mildred muttered desperately to herself.

Lewis checked his watch: 2:13 p.m. They'd been walking for over an hour and had covered very little ground.

Behind Mildred, Annabelle's face burned and she gritted her teeth. She felt absolutely ridiculous carrying a stuffed lamb named Harold. It was outrageous! Humiliating! Worse yet, Dahlia made sure she walked as close behind her as she could, peppering her with instruction.

"Please don't hold Harold upside down . . . or too tightly . . . or by only one leg."

Annabelle swung her arm and Harold with it to scare Dahlia even more.

"Oh, don't swing him so," Dahlia pleaded. "He's quite old and can't be treated roughly!"

Annabelle had had enough. She turned around and yelled, "Stop talking to me!" She next shoved Harold in her pocket so that his legs went every which way. "And stop being such a baby!"

Dahlia's eyes flashed. "I'm not a baby!"

"You are too!" Annabelle shouted. "Whoever heard of a girl your age acting like this over a ratty old stuffed animal—it's ridiculous!"

Dahlia gasped. How could anyone call her a baby? She'd been all on her own for three whole weeks this summer. She'd been blown through the air and had come down in a forest, then hiked to where she'd been offered worms by the bird whose nest she shared for two weeks, then she'd trekked all the way up a mountain to find Mt.

Everbest's Academy for Boys of Busy Parents. She'd become an Everbest Boy! She was loaded with grit! "I'm *not* a baby!" Dahlia shouted.

"Oh yes you are." Annabelle marched off in exasperation.

Dahlia felt terrible. The words stung, and she had to wonder: Was she a baby? Maybe she didn't have as much grit as she thought she did. She felt very sorry for herself . . . as if she didn't have a friend in the world.

Behind Dahlia, Bea was exasperated as well and finally believed that Ms. Rapscott had been right: This semester *was* going to be more difficult than the last. "Can't you go any faster, Mildred?" she pleaded, but Bea was so far behind she didn't know if Mildred could even hear her. Bea repeated, "Mildred! Can't you go *any* faster?"

Mildred was trying, but didn't Bea know she was going as fast as she could?

"MILDRED!" Bea barked even louder.

"I-I can't go faster!" Mildred panted. The worse she felt the harder it was to hurry. *Oh, Bea*

*will never want to be my friend after this ... proba-
bly no one will,* Mildred thought miserably.

Bea couldn't stand being in the back, being last, going slow. She wanted to push everyone out of her way, rush ahead, take the lead, and get out of this awful cave. "MILDRED! HURRY UP!" she yelled dangerously loud, and the others covered their ears.

Meanwhile, the ride in the barrel plus all the day's activity, coupled with being yelled at, had taken its toll on the chubby red-haired girl. Her face was bright red; her breath was ragged. "I-I can't go any faster!" Mildred cried. Then she slowed even more to a snail's pace.

Bea couldn't take it anymore and forgot about everything she'd learned last semester at school. She erupted into an earsplitting explosion that reverberated off the walls of the cave and might have been heard all the way back to the lighthouse.

"*HURRY UP, MILDRED!!*" she bellowed.

"I *can't*," Mildred cried, and crumpled to the ground.

The girls quickly gathered around her.

Annabelle held both arms out and let them drop. "Now, look what you've done," she scolded Bea.

What *had* she done, Bea worried, and glanced at Ms. Rapscott to see if she was in trouble.

Ms. Rapscott remained unfazed—jolly even. "Things are worse than I could have ever imagined!" She seemed very pleased and leaned over her sobbing student. "Mildred? Does anything hurt?"

"N-n-o-o-o-o-o," Mildred wailed.

"Your feet don't hurt?" Ms. Rapscott asked sympathetically. "Or your finger, or your nose, or your pinkie toe, or an elbow, perhaps?"

"No. No. No-o-o-o-o." Mildred cried even harder.

Ms. Rapscott pressed the girl for what was wrong. "Do you feel sad?"

Mildred sat up and used the back of her hand to wipe her tear-streaked face. "Yes."

Ms. Rapscott turned to the others and wiggled her eyebrows. "We're getting somewhere, class." She continued questioning Mildred. "Is it that you suspect nobody likes you?"

"Y-y-y-es." Mildred's lower lip trembled uncontrollably.

Ms. Raspcott's eyes lit up, and she spoke more forcibly. "And do you feel that you haven't a friend in the world?"

Mildred nodded several times. "Yes—that's it."

"It's just as I thought!" Ms. Rapscott exclaimed excitedly.

"What is?" the girls crowded in closer, eager to hear.

"It's a case of Hurt Feelings—the worst I've ever seen!" Ms. Rapscott announced.

"Ms. Rapscott?" Dahlia tugged on the headmistress's sleeve. "I think I've got Hurt Feelings, too."

Ms. Rapscott's face fell, "Oh *no*, Dahlia, not you *too*."

"Yes, I think so," Dahlia said. "I'm quite certain none of the girls likes me . . . and I feel like I haven't a friend in the world—not even Harold anymore."

"You might be right, Dahlia." The headmistress examined the tiny girl's face for more symptoms and turned to Lewis and Clark "There it is, right, boys? The telltale lackluster sheen to her eyes."

The corgis nodded sadly, for all the signs were there.

"Really?" Dahlia said in a weak voice. Without Harold she wasn't surprised that her eyes were lackluster.

Ms. Rapscott studied Dahlia's appearance and recognized something else. "There's also the classic slump to your shoulders—tell me, Dahlia, have you also been feeling sorry for yourself lately?"

"Now that you mention it, I have," Dahlia replied.

Ms. Rapscott shook her head. "Oh, it's worse than I thought—*two* students with Hurt Feelings." Lewis shook his head, too, and his tail drooped. So did Clark's.

"But surely there's a cure," Annabelle asked tensely.

Ms. Rapscott once more leaned over Mildred, who had ceased crying. She had been so interested in Dahlia's problems that she'd all but forgotten about her own. "Have you been feeling sorry for yourself, too, Mildred?"

Reminded of her woes, Mildred collapsed to the ground again and cried, "Ye-he-he-he-hessss!"

Ms. Rapscott sighed with resignation. "I'm afraid there's nothing more we can do for either one of these girls. It's very hard to leave The Bottom with this bad a case of Hurt Feelings." The headmistress brushed off her hands. Then she and her corgis started down the path again. "We'll just have to carry on without Mildred and Dahlia! Come along, class," she called over her shoulder.

Annabelle was flabbergasted to think that the teacher would leave two students at The Bottom!

But it was Bea who said, "We can't leave Mildred down here."

Ms. Rapscott stopped to reconsider. "Hmmm. They might improve . . . but they will never make it to The Top feeling sorry for themselves." Ms. Rapscott walked away. "So we may as well go. Come along, girls!"

"WAIT!" Bea shouted. She knelt down next to Mildred and said, "Please don't cry."

Annabelle took Harold from her pocket and showed him to Dahlia. "See? You *do* have *one* friend."

Just seeing Harold and how bedraggled he looked from his ordeal in Annabelle's pocket made Dahlia's eyes fill with tears, and even though she tried to summon as much grit as she could, it was no use and she too began to cry. Mildred's shoulders shook and she cried even harder. "I'm an aw-aw-aw-awful leader."

"No you're not." Bea straightened Mildred's hard hat that had become lopsided on her head. "You just need more practice."

"I-I do?" Mildred hiccupped.

"Sure," Bea said. "It's not hard at all to lead— all you have to do is be first."

"I hadn't thought of it that way," Mildred sniffed.

Bea was sure she could see the lackluster sheen going away and a little sparkle coming back into Mildred's eyes.

Annabelle exhaled loudly because Dahlia Thistle still looked like she had Hurt Feelings. "Oh, for heaven's sake, Dahlia," she said impatiently. "I don't *really* think you're a baby."

"You don't?" Dahlia sniffled.

Annabelle gave Dahlia a sidelong look and straightened the stuffed lamb's legs out and smoothed his fur. "After all, you did find your own way last semester."

Dahlia stood up a little taller. "That's true."

"You even lived in a nest for a time," Annabelle admitted.

"I almost had to eat worms, too," Dahlia added.

Annabelle's stomach turned at the thought. As much as she disliked this new girl, she couldn't leave her at the bottom of a coal mine—even if the girl did wear her hair like those revolting

Everbest Boys and probably had squishy damp hands. Annabelle said firmly, "Look, I'll be nicer to Harold, okay?"

Dahlia nodded okay and Lewis offered her a tissue. She blew her nose and dried her eyes.

"I won't yell at you anymore," Bea promised Mildred.

Mildred stopped crying. "I'll try to go faster." Then she took a deep breath and squared her shoulders.

"A miraculous recovery!" Ms. Rapscott was very pleased. "It takes a true Rapscott Girl to be able to cure such a bad case of Hurt Feelings."

Bea and Annabelle were pleased to be called true Rapscott Girls but also relieved that they weren't going to have to leave Mildred and Dahlia there in the coal mine.

For the first time, Mildred smiled at Dahlia and Dahlia smiled back.

Mildred took up the lead once more and was encouraged that the farther they went the less rocky and easier it became to walk.

Dahlia was inspired by Mildred's determination to continue and this time she found enough grit to go on without Harold.

Annabelle put him back in her pocket, careful to arrange him in a more comfortable position.

The path now rose steadily before the girls. Light streamed in, and they all turned off their headlamps. Mildred's spirits rose as well. Though she was exhausted and her legs felt like lead, she pushed herself to march along, and when they turned the corner the narrow confines of the coal mine had abruptly opened up to a cavernous room.

A dim magical light shone down from a hole in the cave's ceiling and rested on a little boat that listed to one side in a shallow underground lake. "Look, everyone!" Mildred splashed through the water to it. Sure enough, when the girls got closer they could see the boat's name written across the stern:

THE EXIT

Bea, Mildred, Annabelle, and Dahlia were tired and hungry and covered from head to toe in coal dust. Their bellies were empty and their feet were wet from the ride in the barrel, but Bea, Mildred, Annabelle, and Dahlia didn't mind.

In fact, they'd never felt better.

Chapter 8

Fay Fails in the Best Possible Way

In fine Rapscott Girl fashion Mildred used a rope ladder that hung over the side of the boat to climb aboard. The others followed and were relieved when they saw the inside of the snug little cabin. The walls were made of knotty pine. There was a large wooden wheel for steering and round portholes for looking out. There was a built-in berth with a thick blue-and-yellow Scotch-plaid cushion and a copper kettle on top of a fat red woodstove.

As soon as Dahlia shut the cabin door behind her the boat lurched to one side.

Ms. Rapscott and the girls scurried to a porthole to see water rushing in below through a gap in the side of the cave. The boat tipped and the girls fell in a heap on the floor.

"Hang on, class!" Ms. Rapscott grabbed the teakettle and clung on to the wheel, while Lewis hung on to her, and Clark held on to Lewis. The boat spun around and around in the water that lifted them ever higher. From where they crouched the girls could feel themselves rising above The Bottom! When they peeked out the portholes they were sailing through the opening at the top of the cave. Lewis and Clark grabbed the wheel and steered expertly out to sea. Soon they were once again in the midst of angry Hurricane Bertha.

Bea, Mildred, Annabelle, and Dahlia tried to stay calm as the boat dipped and soared over the waves.

Ms. Rapscott remained cheerful. "Boots off!" she ordered.

The girls also peeled off their coal-covered overalls and then settled all in a row on the soft blue-and-yellow cushioned seat.

Meanwhile, Lewis took over the steering of the boat, and Clark fired up the stove.

"Slippers on! Pillows and blankets out, too, girls!" the teacher commanded.

The girls were soon in their comfy slippers, lying under their blue Rapscott blankets with their pillows behind them.

Ms. Rapscott set out all the lunch things. There was one sardine sandwich with chopped onion and mustard on pumpernickel for her, and two egg salads on rye with the crusts cut off for Lewis and Clark. For the girls there was a choice of tuna with pickles; chicken salad with walnuts; bacon, lettuce, and tomato; and peanut butter and jelly; and of course birthday cake for dessert.

"Mugs out! Hot chocolate, too!" Ms. Rapscott poured steaming water from the teakettle into each of their cups as well as her own and the corgis. Then she settled into an easy chair in the corner.

Bertha blew the boat up one wave and down another. Rain thrashed the sides of the cabin and the wind whistled. All the while the little stove burned brightly and the girls were glad to be inside. But once they finished their sandwiches and started on dessert, their thoughts turned to their missing classmate whom they dearly hoped was not outside in this storm.

Bea asked Ms. Rapscott the question that was on everyone's mind: "Is Fay all right?"

"Let's see." The headmistress went to a porthole to look out through her binoculars. "Aha! I knew that girl would go far!"

"Do you see her?" the girls all asked at once.

"I see her as clear as the nose on my face," Ms. Rapscott exclaimed. "Fay is at The Top!"

"The Top?" Bea said puzzled. "How did she get there?"

"By mistake," Ms. Rapscott pronounced. "Fay has failed in the best possible way."

"Impossible!" Annabelle exclaimed.

"But true." Ms. Rapscott took her seat in the easy chair once more. "Her box was shipped straight to The Top by mistake."

"But this is so unfair!" Bea sputtered. "Why

didn't Fay have to start at The Bottom like us? Why did she get to go straight to The Top?"

"Yeah!" Mildred, Dahlia, and even Annabelle agreed.

"We have to go get her," Bea said, perturbed.

"Oh, no, when you're at The Top you never want to leave," Ms. Rapscott said knowingly. "If we took Fay from The Top now it would ruin everything for her."

"Good!" Bea snapped.

"But why would we ruin things for Fay, Ms. Rapscott?" Mildred asked. "Is it really that great?"

"It is." Ms. Rapscott grinned broadly. "Fay would've been greeted with fireworks, a red carpet to walk down, and a box of chocolate-covered cherries wrapped up with a gold bow!" Ms. Rapscott winked. "When you are at The Top people give you anything you want."

Mildred liked the idea of that. "Will Fay get her own giant TV in her own room, too, Ms. Rapscott?"

"If she wants," Ms. Rapscott replied.

"Will Fay get a pony or a parakeet?" Dahlia

asked. She'd always wanted both, but of course her parents were too busy for pets.

"As many as Fay wants," Ms. Rapscott said.

Bea thought for a moment and then said, "Do people listen to you at The Top?"

"With bated breath, Bea," Ms. Rapscott said.

"Even if you whisper?" Bea whispered.

"They will strain their ears to hear!" Ms. Rapscott said.

Bea wished that she was Fay right now. "Fay's so lucky."

Ms. Rapscott remained silent and just raised an eyebrow.

"Did you ever make it to The Top?" Dahlia asked.

"I tried once, but I failed," the headmistress admitted. She finished her birthday cake and put her feet up on the footstool. The rain pummeled the cabin, and the corgis steered the little boat nimbly over the waves and across the choppy ocean.

"It's a very difficult thing to reach The Top, class," Ms. Rapscott mused.

The girls pulled their blankets tightly around themselves and sipped their hot chocolate as they listened to Ms. Rapscott tell her story.

"It happened not long after I came to the lighthouse. I was very young back then and all I knew was that I wanted to Go Far in Life, but I wasn't sure which way to go. Then I heard about The Top. I heard that it was very far away in a castle in the clouds, and I could have whatever my heart desired there. That sounded good to me, so I decided to try to get there. Every day I walked down the sandy road to the hills and practiced going up them. Beyond the hills were the mountains. As I got stronger I could easily climb them as well. Soon I felt ready. I packed all the crackers, cheese, and hot chocolate I could carry and started out. The farther I went, the more I knew I just *had* to get to The Top. It was thrilling! But the longer I walked the more distant it seemed and after many months I finally ran out of crackers. Then cheese. Then hot chocolate. The road I was on came to an end by the sea as well."

"Were you scared?" Bea asked, because Ms. Rapscott never seemed to get scared, no matter what.

"Of course I was scared! Worse yet, when I turned around I saw I'd gone right by The Top without even knowing it. I said to myself, You've gone too far, Ms. Rapscott!"

"Can you go too far?" Dahlia had never heard of such a thing.

"Yes, Dahlia. I had *failed* to realize this and when I did it was too late."

Ms. Rapscott put her cup down, folded her arms, and looked the girls straight in the eye to let that sink in.

"Well? What did you do?" Bea asked.

"I was more tired than I'd ever been in my entire life, and I just laid down and fell into a deep sleep right where I was. I dreamed that I was being carried back over the mountains, ever so gently, over hills and then down the sandy roads. When I woke up I was at the lighthouse in a bed that was like a boat." Ms. Rapscott nodded knowingly but would say no more.

"But, Ms. Rapscott, how?" Bea asked.

"Was it magic?" Mildred wanted to know.

"Were you rescued?" Annabelle demanded.

"Who carried you?" Dahlia wondered.

But Ms. Rapscott wouldn't say. She went over and gazed out the porthole, and when she turned to face the girls there was a sparkle in her eye. "There is no need for us to go and get Fay. Instead we will *meet* her at The Top!"

"Can we go now?" Bea asked excitedly.

"Patience, Bea," Ms. Rapscott warned. "You must all cultivate patience, girls, if you ever want to reach The Top, for it's a mysterious place. Some people can struggle their entire lives, certain that they are almost there, only to be turned away. Then again, some find themselves there quite by surprise. But for most it takes time and patience."

"But we made it to The Bottom," Bea persisted.

"You made lots of mistakes and the trip was a complete success!" Ms. Rapscott said proudly.

"So why can't we go now?" Bea pressed, and the others wanted to know as well.

"Because there are more lessons for you to learn," Ms. Rapscott replied.

No matter how much they pestered the teacher she wouldn't budge. "Look, girls!" she exclaimed.

When they looked out the portholes, too, off in the distance there was the lighthouse, shining out as far as the eye could see, and they were back at school.

Chapter 9
HEAD GIRL

The next morning Bea, Mildred, Annabelle, and Dahlia were awakened by thunder that shook them in their beds. The girls peeked out to see the windows of their dorm streaked with rain.

Ms. Rapscott tripped lightly down the spiral stairs, seemingly unfazed by the furious storm outside. "A new hurricane has begun, class." She and the corgis entered the dorm wearing long navy blue and white quilted robes over their flannel pajamas to ward off the chill. "Today Hurricane Bessie—Known for Being Thunderous—will be visiting us."

Lewis carried a tray with cups of steaming hot chocolate. Clark followed around the room handing them out.

"This morning I will announce who will be Head Girl," Ms. Rapscott said brightly. Once the hot chocolate was delivered, the headmistress and her corgis trotted back up the stairs. "Morning Meeting is at eight o'clock sharp!" she called from the floor above.

Bea emptied her cup and was the first one out of bed. She was very excited because she knew she would be Head Girl. She'd been the first one to do everything yesterday and had even cured Mildred of her Hurt Feelings. Ms. Rapscott had to pick her! She couldn't wait to be Head Girl so that she could tell everyone what to do and they'd all have to listen to her.

Annabelle threw back the covers of her bed and sighed. As the only student with a lick of common sense she thought she was the obvious choice to be Head Girl. It definitely wouldn't be Fay, who wasn't even here because she was living it up at The Top. It wouldn't be Mildred or Dahlia—what with that display of Hurt Feelings yesterday. The only other contender was Bea. For the most part Bea had stopped being Loud, but now she always had to be first and it was almost as annoying. Annabelle rolled her eyes to think how even more annoying Bea would act if she became Head Girl. Annabelle suddenly hoped, if for no reason other than to keep Bea from being Head Girl, that Ms. Rapscott would pick her for the job.

Mildred lay in her bed wondering as well about who would most likely be Head Girl. She knew for sure it would not be her. Yesterday's events roared back into her mind, and she cringed to think that she'd almost gotten left at The Bottom because of having Hurt Feelings. At least she wasn't the only one. Dahlia Thistle had almost been left there, too, and she even had grit. Mildred followed Dahlia down the stairs to the bathroom.

Dahlia immediately did something wrong.

"That's Fay's sink," Bea said coldly.

Dahlia moved to the only other unoccupied one. At Mt. Everbest her toothbrush and toothpaste were in a cabinet behind the mirror. But here at Great Rapscott the cabinet was empty.

Dahlia asked Annabelle, "Where's my tooth-brush?" But Annabelle was busy getting dressed and acted like she didn't hear.

Dahlia asked Mildred, but she was busy brush-ing her teeth and didn't answer.

Dahlia asked Bea as well, but Bea was busy drying her hair and didn't answer, either.

Of course this was very rude behavior but typical of girls of busy parents. They had been ignored all their lives because their parents were busy, so the girls in turn ignored others when-ever they got busy!

Girls of busy parents are also known for be-ing very protective of their own things because they never learned How to Share. Bea had made sure she put her shampoo and dental floss on the highest shelf where Dahlia couldn't reach them. Similarly, Annabelle had hid her shower cap and toenail clippers under the sink.

Dahlia was used to being on her own. She'd been left at the mall, the grocery store, even the Department of Motor Vehicles once because her parents were so busy they forgot all about her, but she'd never felt so lost or lonely. She knew she was tiny, but now it was as if she had become invisible, too; the other girls acted as if she wasn't even there!

It was getting later and later, and she hadn't even washed her hands because she couldn't find a bar of soap or a towel. She panicked, looking wildly around and wondering what to do next. Why, the very sight of this bewildered small girl desperate for the most minor of things—a mere toothbrush and a dab of toothpaste—would have plucked at the heartstrings of most, but Bea and Annabelle had also never learned How to Feel Sorry for Someone Besides Themselves.

Of course, Mildred had felt sorry for herself many times, especially yesterday. From her side of the bathroom she watched Dahlia, who stood motionless in the middle of the bathroom. The circles under her eyes looked even darker—like smudges of charcoal—and she looked even smaller and more fragile than usual.

Suddenly there was a flash of lightning. It lit up the bathroom, followed quickly by a deafening clap of thunder from Hurricane Bessie. Mildred stopped right in the middle of brushing her teeth, and toothpaste dripped out of her mouth and off her chin.

If she could feel sorry for herself, could she feel sorry for someone else? Mildred blinked her eyes. Wait . . . did she feel *sorry* for Dahlia Thistle? Could it be?

She looked closely in the mirror to check to see if she was still herself. Yes, she was still herself, and she *did* feel sorry for Dahlia Thistle!

Maybe, Mildred thought, *I can do something . . . maybe . . . I can help Dahlia Thistle!* Mildred quickly wiped her mouth with a towel.

"Dahlia!" Mildred pointed to the corner cabinet. "That's where the soap, toothbrushes, and toothpaste are." Next Mildred took Dahlia to the linen closet. "Here are where all your towels are."

Dahlia gave Mildred a relieved smile and thanked her several times.

"And if you need anything else just tell Clark and he will get it for you," Mildred explained.

Dahlia was grateful and thanked Mildred once again, then hurried off to get ready for Morning Meeting. Mildred no longer had to feel sorry for her and felt much *much* better.

The exchange between Mildred and Dahlia had not gone unnoticed.

Girls of busy parents don't have many friends—but like their shower caps and toenail clippers they don't like to share the few friends they have, either.

Bea watched with alarm from across the room. Mildred was *her* friend, not Dahlia Thistle's. Why was Mildred being so nice to the new girl?

Annabelle noticed, too, and was surprised, but she didn't care as much as Bea. Of all the girls Annabelle was slowest to form friendships and still considered the other girls mere acquaintances, which is how it is when you are Old for Your Age. As far as she was concerned, Mildred could be as friendly with this new girl as she wanted, but Annabelle didn't want Dahlia Thistle touching her things with her squishy damp hands.

Annabelle rubbed her eyeglasses vigorously with a tissue and then placed them deliberately on her nose. Bea checked the angle of her hat in the mirror, and then they hurried downstairs to Morning Meeting to see who would be Head Girl.

When all the girls were seated in the classroom, Clark passed out birthday cake and ice cream. Ms. Rapscott lit the candles, and they all made their wishes.

Bea wished she would be picked as Head Girl.

Mildred wished that she would keep up better on the next adventure.

Annabelle still thought wishes were childish.

Dahlia wished that she could be Head Girl, too, and that maybe the other girls would be nice to her now like Mildred had.

Lewis checked his watch against the clock on the wall and nodded.

Clark rapped the chalkboard with his pointer to get their attention.

Ms. Rapscott stood next to a chalk drawing of a birthday cake five tiers high. On each tier was a piece of paper that covered a girl's name.

With a flick of the wrist Ms. Rapscott swiped off the bottom covering and called out, "Fay! She's not here to be Head Girl."

The girls held their breath as the headmistress moved up the drawing of the cake to the next name.

Mildred looked down guiltily because it was her. "I'm sorry, Ms. Rapscott."

"You went home, Mildred, for six weeks and forgot everything you learned here at Great Rapscott School," Ms. Rapscott scolded.

Mildred was on the verge of tears. "I know."

"If you do that again, you will not be sent home for a long, long time!"

Mildred thought about it. As much as she loved her parents, they were never home. Now Mildred was in no hurry to go back. "I won't be sent home?" she said hopefully.

"No, you'll stay right here!" Ms. Rapscott made a little hop and Clark grinned. Before the other girls could comment about not being sent home, too, Ms. Rapscott plucked off the third paper with a flourish. "Annabelle!"

Annabelle stuck out her lower lip and frowned.

"You must try harder to act your age, Annabelle." Ms. Rapscott waggled a finger at the girl.

"Act my age?" Annabelle groaned. "But how?"

The headmistress thought for a moment and then made a little check mark in the air with her index finger. "You might try jumping rope!"

"What's that?" Annabelle asked.

"Or hide-and-seek? Or perhaps you could build a tree house!" Ms. Rapscott liked all these ideas. So did Clark, and he wrote them down.

Of course Annabelle had no idea how to do any of these things because she'd never learned How to Play. She was always too busy at home looking after her parents who were too busy to look after themselves.

"It's what's known as *playing*, Annabelle," Ms. Rapscott said. "Girls your age do it all the time."

Annabelle tried to think if she'd read about this in the *Encyclopedia Britannica* and decided she hadn't. "Playing?"

"To have *fun*," Ms. Rapscott replied.

Annabelle pulled in her chin and frowned.

"Ms. Rapscott." Dahlia held up her hand. "I think I had fun once."

"Tell us, Dahlia." Ms. Rapscott smiled.

"There was this time that my father's assistant's wife's daughter took me to a department store, and because she was so busy she lost me there. So a security guard found me and took me to the offices upstairs, and they let me color with crayons—that's fun, right?"

"Precisely, Dahlia!" Ms. Rapscott exclaimed. Then she pulled off the second to last paper and Bea's face fell.

"Excellent job, Bea," Ms. Rapscott said.

"But, Ms. Rapscott!" Bea cried. "Why aren't I at the top?"

"You're almost at the top," the headmistress said smoothly.

"Not the tippy-top." Bea was extremely upset. She'd been first all day yesterday—it wasn't fair.

Ms. Rapscott's nostrils flared slightly, she raised an eyebrow and drew one corner of her mouth to the side the way she did whenever she began to sense trouble coming. "I fear, Bea, that you are becoming Known for Always Having to Be First."

"But what's wrong with that?" Bea didn't understand.

"It can be quite tiring, Bea. You must learn to pace yourself," Ms. Rapscott replied. She closed her eyes and held up one finger. "Like the proud turtle, class, slow and steady often wins the race."

"That's right, Bea," Mildred said smugly, delighted by this novel idea that being poky wasn't so bad after all.

"Humph," said Bea, feeling very misunderstood.

Ms. Rapscott revealed the last name with a flick of the wrist.

"Excellent job, Dahlia Thistle!" Ms. Rapscott said.

"Yay, Dahlia!" Mildred yelled and clapped. But when she looked around neither Bea nor Annabelle shared in her enthusiasm. Bea in particular glared at her, so Mildred stopped clapping and became quiet.

"But she had Hurt Feelings," Bea protested.

Ms. Rapscott dismissed the remark with a wave of her hand. "It takes a true Rapscott Girl to rise above The Bottom after such a bad case of Hurt Feelings!"

Lewis and Clark stepped forward to shake Dahlia's hand.

"Congratulations, Dahlia, you will be our new Head Girl for the entire semester!"

Dahlia couldn't believe her ears.

"The entire semester?" Bea smacked her forehead with the palm of her hand. The summer session had only been three weeks, but Bea had been named Head Girl the first week and Mildred had won the title the second. "But we had two Head Girls last semester!"

Annabelle's hopes of becoming Head Girl this semester had been dashed as well. She waved her hand vigorously and called out, "Bea is right, Ms. Rapscott! We had two Head Girls!"

"That's because it was our introductory summer program," Ms. Rapscott replied. "During the fall semester there is never any more than one Head Girl. Ever."

Bea muttered, "So unfair."

Annabelle huffed.

Ms. Rapscott paid no attention to either girl. "It's a big responsibility, Dahlia. I have high expectations for you to be a leader and a role model of good behavior!"

Dahlia sat a little taller in her seat. She wasn't used to being the center of attention. In fact she wasn't used to any attention. Mildred caught Dahlia's eye to give her a thumbs-up, and Dahlia smiled back. But it was too much for Bea and Annabelle to bear. They both sat with sour expressions on their faces, neither even trying to hide how they felt, and Bea vowed that she was absolutely going to be *not* nice to the new Head Girl.

Ms. Rapscott strode over to the map, pulled on the string, and rolled it down like a window shade. "The Top!" She pointed to a spot on the map. "Fay is right here, class."

"It looks far." Mildred shivered a little to think that they would have to travel all the way there.

"Oh, it's *very* far!" Ms. Rapscott said, pleased because she loved a long trip. "There is much to learn, but I believe we will be ready to go by your birthday, Mildred."

"When is that?" Bea looked to Mildred.

Mildred lowered her eyes. She didn't know. Her parents had always been too busy to tell her.

"Mildred's birthday is in two weeks," Ms. Rapscott said.

Just then there was a sudden crack of thunder, and all the girls jumped in their seats. There was another loud *BOOM!* Then the rain came down in torrents, pounding at the walls of the lighthouse, and peels of thunder almost jolted them out of their seats.

Mildred had to shout to make herself heard. "Is it always this way in hurricane season?"

"Always!" Ms. Rapscott shouted back. "Never forget, girls! Life is like a hurricane. It twirls you around, knocks you off your feet and can blow you into unfamiliar territory, but you must always just put on your rain bonnet and enjoy the ride!"

"Sorta like being carried out to sea in a barrel, right, Ms. Rapscott?" Bea added.

"A barrel?" Ms. Rapscott asked.

Mildred spoke up. "Like yesterday when the mayor came by? In the barrel?"

"I don't know what either of you two girls is talking about," Ms. Rapscott said. "Lewis? Clark? What's this about barrels?"

The corgis just shrugged and there was no further talk about it.

Chapter 10

THE SEVENTH FLOOR

The girls fell into the routine of life at Great Rapscott School and it quickly became clear—even to Bea—that this semester would be harder than the last. For one thing there was far more schoolwork to do. There were also tests every Monday, Wednesday, and Friday on all the things that they learned on Tuesdays, Thursdays, and Saturdays. Even at lunch Clark took notes and the girls were graded on discussions about essential things their parents were too busy to teach their daughters like: how to use a can opener, shine shoes, and get rid of ants.

True to her vow Bea was doing her best to be not nice to Dahlia Thistle. She tried to do this at least three times a day. In the morning when she first climbed out of bed, Bea made it a habit to say hello to Mildred and Annabelle but not Dahlia. At lunch Bea always talked about all the things that had happened last semester so that Dahlia would feel really left out. At night, when the hurricanes were at their worst and it sounded like the lighthouse would be picked up and blown away, Bea invited everyone except Dahlia to sit on her bed. Bea enjoyed seeing Dahlia sitting all by herself. Being not nice to Dahlia Thistle always made Bea feel better.

Not Mildred. On those stormy nights Mildred would ask, "What about Dahlia?"

"There's no room," Bea always said until Mildred eventually stopped asking. Then one night a terrible hurricane blew in with winds that howled and waves that pounded and shook the lighthouse so violently that Dahlia Thistle was actually thrown from her bed and landed *SPLAT!* on the floor. Mildred ran to help the girl and pick up Harold, who'd fallen hard on his head and was lying in a heap in the corner.

Once again, Bea called to Mildred to wait out

the storm on her bed. But Mildred couldn't help feeling sorry for the new girl and her stuffed lamb, Harold, who'd taken such a bad spill.

"That's okay," Mildred called back to Bea. "I'm going to keep Dahlia company."

And then when the next storm hit, Mildred called to Dahlia, "Come sit on my bed—and bring Harold!"

Bea fumed.

Toward the end of the first week of school, just after ten o'clock at night, Bea was sitting in her blue bed with her notebook propped up on her knees. They'd been given essays to write and she was still working on hers: "Lint: or Never Put Black Tights in the Dryer with White Towels."

Bea couldn't concentrate. She chewed on her pencil, her eyes fixed on the bed next to hers where Mildred and Dahlia sat jabbering away. They both had their noses stuck in some book. Bea frowned. Even though she'd apologized and had practically "saved" Mildred's life at The Bottom, Bea felt like Mildred liked Dahlia better than she liked her now. *Probably because Dahlia is Head Girl*, Bea thought.

"Did you finish your essay, Mildred?" Bea asked.

Mildred didn't answer.

Bea raised her voice. "I *said* . . . did you finish your essay yet, Mildred?"

There was still no answer. Mildred and Dahlia continued to talk. Are they talking about me? Bea suddenly wondered with horror, Is Mildred telling Dahlia that I'm not being nice to her on purpose?

"Mildred?!" Bea shouted angrily.

Mildred poked her head around the bed curtain. "You don't have to shout, Bea!" Mildred said just as angrily.

Bea's face was red with frustration. "I've asked you three times—did you finish your essay?"

Mildred's essay was on the uses of distilled white vinegar. She and Dahlia hadn't been talking about Bea at all, they'd been poring over a curious little book from Ms. Rapscott's shelves.

"Listen to this, Bea," Mildred said, forgetting her annoyance. "It says here: *'Distilled white vinegar can unclog drains, remove candle wax, shine silver . . . trap fruit flies . . .'*"

"SHHHH," Annabelle was busy writing her essay on "How Not to Stub Your Toe."

"But you should hear this, Annabelle," Mildred said excitedly.

Annabelle exhaled loudly. She was right in the middle of a sentence about how you should never get up in the middle of the night to go to the bathroom without first putting on your slippers.

Mildred read, *"'Place 3½ drops of distilled white vinegar on the beak of a bird, and it will give you a precise weather forecast for the next three and a half days.'"*

"Oh, that's helpful," Annabelle said in a voice that meant it really wasn't helpful at all. "And how're you supposed to get the bird to stand still while you put vinegar on his beak?"

"What book is that?" Bea leaned over the side of her bed to see.

Mildred showed her the cover. "It's called, *Everyday and Unusual Useful Uses for Distilled White Vinegar.*" Mildred pointed to the first page of the book. "It says right here: '*No matter what your problem, distilled white vinegar can solve it*'!"

"If you drink some now, will it make you stop talking about distilled white vinegar?" Annabelle put her notebook on the nightstand, finished with her work for the night.

"Ha-ha." Mildred was not amused. "I don't care what you think—from now on I'm bringing distilled white vinegar with me everywhere I go."

"Good for you, Mildred." Bea got under the covers. "Isn't your best friend, our Head Girl, supposed to make sure that lights are out by ten?"

"Yeah!" Annabelle agreed.

"You're right," Dahlia mumbled, and hopped off Mildred's bed. It was so nice to finally have someone to talk to that she'd forgotten all about the time.

"Lights-out," Dahlia tried to say with as much authority as she thought a Head Girl should.

Bea sighed and switched off the lamp on her nightstand—it was so irritating to have to be ordered around by Dahlia Thistle.

The four girls lay in the dark listening to the latest hurricane. It was Hurricane Birdie, Known for Her Whistling Winds. All day long Birdie had been whistling a different tune every few hours. But now the tone of the winds had turned ominous. They blew in through cracks in the windows and made spooky harmonica sounds.

Mildred shivered.

Bea gazed up at the ceiling and her thoughts turned to the mystery three flights up. "I wonder what there could be on the seventh floor," she said.

"Probably a horrible monster," Annabelle called out. "Or maybe a giant spider in a cage!"

"Stop it! You're scaring Harold." Mildred knew he'd been through a lot: shrunk by Mr. Everbest, squished inside Annabelle's pocket, and tossed on his head during a storm. She felt sorry for him and was starting to grow fond of the stuffed lamb.

"Harold is an inanimate object," Annabelle said. "He does not feel scared—ever."

"Yes he does!" Mildred and Dahlia shouted.

"OH!" Annabelle turned her back to the wall. "I'm going to sleep!"

"Well, I think it's a room full of candy," Mildred said, trying to forget about the spider so she wouldn't have bad dreams. "Or birthday cakes," she added.

"Maybe it's Ms. Rapscott's salon where she goes to get her hair done," Bea suggested, since her parents had one of their own on the top floor of their house.

Annabelle rolled back over to say, "Ms. Rapscott is too practical to get her hair done, or her nails done, or anything else done—furthermore I know what's on the seventh floor!"

"What?" the three girls said at the same time.

"It's a fabulous library," Annabelle replied. "Now good night!" With that she rolled over and within a minute was snoring softly.

But Bea, Mildred, and Dahlia lay awake for some time, listening to hurricane Birdie's strange whistling winds and wondering what on earth could be up there on the seventh floor.

With Ms. Rapscott you just never knew.

Chapter 11
Fay's Friendly Letter

The girls were well into their second week of the semester when Ms. Rapscott bustled into the classroom for Morning Meeting waving a piece of paper in her hand. Lewis and Clark trotted briskly behind, their eyes brighter than usual.

"Excellent news, girls!" the headmistress exclaimed. "It's a Friendly Letter from Fay!"

Bea, Mildred, Annabelle, and Dahlia took their seats, eager to hear.

Ms. Rapscott sat behind her desk. She seemed especially pleased with today's hurricane. It was Bobby—Known for Having the Best Winds That Deliver. Sure enough, outside the air was full of packages and letters. They'd been flying about all morning.

"Please, Ms. Rapscott, read it!" Bea called out. Even Annabelle was excited—she couldn't wait to hear about what Fay had been doing all this time.

The windows rattled in their sills as Ms. Rapscott read:

> Dear Ms. ~~Rapscott~~ ~~Rapcott~~ Rapscot (can't spell!!!) Lewis and Clark, Bee, Milderd, Anabell, and Dalia,
>
> As you no I am always doing something ~~wrog~~ wrong . . . well I've done it again!
>
> I was late getting into my box to be shiped to skool and by misstake got sent to the **wrong** place!!!! I'm not exackly sure where I am but I seem to be at sort a Hotel kind a plase called **The Top**?

"Oh brother," Annabelle muttered.
"SHHHH!" Dahlia hissed.

"Don't shush her." Bea stuck her tongue out at Dahlia.

"Girls!" Ms. Rapscott said firmly. When it was quiet the headmistress continued:

I love Great ~~Raspcot~~ rapscot Skool but this is the best plase I've ever been to in my life. I never want to ~~leav haf leafe~~ I want to stay here forever!!! WHY????

I can hav anything I want.

I can do anything I want to do.

Everybody is nise to me here.

I don't have to mop any floors eether.

I'm learning tons to! I found out that I can have this thing called FUN by doing this thing called: "PLAYING." All day long I jus have **Fun Playing!!!**

Here's how: I wake up in my own *beutiful* pink and *purpel* bed in my own pink and *purpel* room and order anything I want for *breakfass.* today

I had grape juice and marcaroni and cheese
with toste and rainbow marmeelade. Then I took
a swiming lessin in the giant pool—there's a
waterfall with a slide that I can go down as many
times as I like—and they say I need to no how to
swim!!! Then I had lunch in a ~~revolving reevolvink
revolving~~ resterant that turns around where I can
order anything I want. Today I had pizza topped
with chokalat chip cukies!!!! Then I took a ride on
the feris wheal thats on the top floor of **The
Top** where you can see forever—I saw the
Great Rapscott lighthouse from there!!!!

But the fun part is that there's so many fun
things to do I never run out. Like there's an entire
room full of costumes and I can dress up like
someone differint everyday. So far I've been a fary
princess, a balerina, a which, and a pirete. I even
have a gold crown with REAL diamons that I can
wear like whenever I want. There's even a **CANDY**
tree that grows in the lobby with **EVRY KIND
OF CANDY** and I can have as much as I want!

There's even a animal called a CORNIHORN—
he's like a horse only he has a sparkly ice cream
cone thing stuck to his forehead and his hoofs are
all gold gliter. His name is Twinkle Toes and **he's
mine!!!!**

Annabelle's hand shot up. "Ms. Rapscott *Ms.
Rapscott*! She means UNICORN! Not cornihorn!"

"SHHHHH!" Dahlia hushed Annabelle crossly
again.

"Annabelle's right, Dahlia," Ms. Rapscott
said. Lewis and Clark nodded in agreement. Annabelle and Bea gave Dahlia smug looks.

Ms. Rapscott read on:

BUT . . . The best part of all is that they say
this place is only for <u>speshile people</u>. I never
thought I was speshile. I thaught all I could ever
do was mop floors and do things wrog—but for
once the thing I did wrog turned out to be right!!!

Anyways I'm writing you late at night from my
bed and I'm geting kind a tired so I'll say good-

bye. Twinkle Toes is cerled up in his bed by the fireplace. Wish you cud see him—hes SO kute!!!!! It's snowing outside but when I turn the lights out the sky is full of sparkly stars. It's beuttifull.

So don't worry about me Ms. Raspcott because the only thing I'm worried about is ever having to leeve this wonderfle plase. There's only one rule I have to remember in order to stay, and that is: ALWAYS BE HAPPY.

I am happy, Ms. Rapscott. Who woun't be?

Your student and freind,
Fay Mandrake

P.s. **Please** write back soon. You have to be so speshile to get to **The Top** that there is hardly anyone else here.

As soon as Ms. Rapscott finished the letter the girls started to talk at once.

Bea was fired up to start off for The Top right away. "We have to go *now*! We have to go *today*!"

"There are no such things as unicorns." Annabelle sniffed.

"A candy tree, yum . . . Oh, The Top sounds wonderful," Mildred said dreamily.

"My own room with a fireplace and my own unicorn." Dahlia sighed.

"Ms. Rapscott!" Bea waved her hand. "When can we go?"

"Patience, Bea," Ms. Rapscott said. "We will go a week from today on Mildred's birthday."

"But why?" Bea groaned, frustrated at having to wait that long.

Ms. Rapscott straightened the papers on her desk. "There are still some things for you to learn first."

"Like what?" Bea asked. "Fay got there without learning anything!" The other girls chimed in to agree.

Ms. Rapscott waited until the room was completely quiet then said, "It can be dangerous to get to The Top too soon."

None of the girls understood because what could be dangerous about getting to a place where you got to dress up like someone different every day and have your own unicorn? And as much candy as you wanted? And your own purple and pink room? It didn't make sense.

Ms. Rapscott's face darkened. "Because," she intoned, "once you reach The Top you have nowhere to go . . . but *down*."

Lewis and Clark nodded to reinforce the headmistress's words.

Ms. Rapscott continued in a somber voice. "It's also *extremely* difficult to stay there because it's very hard to keep the rule."

"Always Be Happy?" Bea asked. "That doesn't sound so hard."

"It doesn't *sound* hard but it is," Ms. Rapscott answered.

Bea rested her chin in her hand and scowled, but she knew there was no use in trying to change Ms. Rapscott's mind.

"The Top can also be a lonely place and we must write back to Fay immediately," Ms. Rapscott said.

Clark hurried to the class supply closet and re-appeared with some paper.

"We will write a Friendly Letter to Fay, class!" Ms. Rapscott announced. The corgi handed her the paper and she held it up. "Here we have *official* Rapscott Friendly Letter Paper."

The girls leaned forward in their seats to see a pretty picture of the lighthouse on cream-colored paper with a blue border.

Ms. Rapscott handed it back to Clark. "Take notes, girls. Take notes."

As soon as the girls picked up their pencils Ms. Raspcott began. "The salutation!" her voice reverberated throughout the room. "Start your Friendly Letter by addressing your friend with a friendly, 'Howdy!' or 'Greetings!' or a simple, 'Hello!' Next, mention the weather or time of year, for example: *I do hope you are having a wonderful hurricane season.*"

The girls scribbled away as Ms. Rapscott spoke. "Next, tell your friend what you are doing and any news you'd like to share. And finally end your letter with something nice, like 'Sincerely,' or, 'Adiós.'" Ms. Rapscott paused and waited until the girls had finished their notes. Clark clipped his Friendly Letter Paper onto his board. He nodded that he was ready and Ms. Rapscott said, "So, let's begin our Friendly Letter to Fay. Anyone?"

Bea had her hand up first. "Howdy, Fay!"

"Very good, Bea," Ms. Rapscott said, pleased, and Clark wrote it down. "Anything else?"

Bea thought for a second and her eyes lit up. "I hope you have a wonderful hurricane season and that you get unhappy soon so you get kicked out of The Top and you can come back to school."

Ms. Rapscott no longer looked pleased. "That's not very friendly, Bea. How about telling Fay of our plan?"

Mildred waved her hand and the words tumbled out of her mouth. "We're coming to meet you on my birthday."

"Good, Mildred." Ms. Rapscott turned to Annabelle. "Anything else?"

"Congratulations for making it to The Top," Annabelle said.

"Nice, Annabelle." Ms. Rapscott was pleasantly

surprised until Annabelle added, "You're a lot more special than I thought—"

"Annabelle," the headmistress said sternly. "That's not very friendly."

"But it's the truth!" Annabelle cried.

Ms. Rapscott waved her hand. "We are trying to be friendly right now, Annabelle, never mind the truth. Any suggestions—Dahlia?"

Dahlia stood to speak. "I hope you can stay at The Top till we get there?"

"Better," Ms. Rapscott said.

Finally Dahlia suggested they end the letter with "Adiós."

"Perfect!" Ms. Rapscott exclaimed. "Sign your names, girls." She sent the letter around for each girl to sign.

Ms. Rapscott had one more thing to say. "I'm going to add something at the end, class." She wrote: *P.S. You have failed in the best possible way, Fay. We always knew you'd go far!"* Then Lewis put it in an envelope. Ms. Rapscott threw open a window where Hurricane Bobby plucked it from her fingers to deliver it right to Fay at The Top.

Chapter 12
How to Take Matters into Your Own Hands

In one week it would be Mildred's birthday and the girls would finally have a chance to try for The Top. Everyone could barely concentrate on their schoolwork like they knew a true Rapscott Girl should.

It was especially difficult for Dahlia. She tried to lead by setting a good example, but it wasn't easy being a Head Girl when you were used to being an Everbest Boy.

Dahlia could make and throw a snowball as fast as the boys. She knew how to hammer a nail and what to feed a gerbil. But Dahlia still couldn't get the knack of how to knot the tie on her uniform and often had to rely on Mildred to do it for her. She also had a terrible time performing even the most basic things, like how to make toast, the proper way to use a Q-Tip, and how to cut bangs—all the things that the other girls had already learned during the first semester. The harder Dahlia tried, the less it seemed that she would ever be a Rapscott Girl. There were so many things she didn't know! She was constantly being corrected for burping loudly after she ate; she was always forgetting to carry tissues; and she had no idea how to buy sneakers.

"She's an awful Head Girl," Bea whispered to Annabelle at lunch one day.

"Oh, I know," Annabelle said. "She doesn't even know How to Pick Out a Good Cantaloupe!"

Dahlia had heard, but she thought Bea and Annabelle were right. "I'm an awful Head Girl," Dahlia whispered to Mildred.

"No, you're not." Mildred fibbed to cheer Dahlia up because she didn't just feel sorry for her anymore—she was actually starting to like her.

By the end of the week Dahlia was weary of her job as Head Girl; Bea and Annabelle were weary of her; Mildred was weary of waiting for her birthday; and they were all ready to go meet Fay at The Top.

The day before Mildred's birthday, the girls were on edge. At lunchtime Ms. Rapscott gathered them around the stove. Lewis cracked several eggs in a bowl, beat them with a fork, and then Clark poured them into a heavy black skillet.

The headmistress breathed deeply through her regal nose and said, "We should all aspire to be like the mighty frying pan, class: made of cast iron and, just like a true Rapscott Girl, if perfectly seasoned should last at least one hundred years!"

Annabelle rolled her eyes and sighed loudly. Ms. Rapscott was always telling her to be like something that she didn't want to be like. Now it was a frying pan.

The girls gazed in complete puzzlement at the eggs as they sizzled and popped.

"Observe, class," Ms. Rapscott said. "The frying pan doesn't say, 'Is it all right if I cook the eggs now, Ms. Rapscott,' does it? It doesn't ask, 'Am I doing this right, Ms. Rapscott?'"

The girls shook their heads even though they weren't at all sure that the frying pan said anything. After all, it didn't have a mouth or even a head.

"The frying pan just cooks the eggs." Ms. Rapscott next took one step to the side and gestured at something on the edge of the sink. "Likewise the all important sponge." She proceeded to wipe up some spilled egg. "Absorbent and dishwasher safe, girls—just like a true Rapscott Girl—but there is far more to the sponge. Much like the frying pan, the sponge doesn't ask permission. It doesn't say, 'Is it time to sop, Ms. Rapscott?' The sponge just sops up whatever comes its way until it can sop no more, class."

Ms. Rapscott paused here and the girls waited. "Any questions?" she asked.

Mildred raised her hand. "I don't get it."

"Don't you see, Mildred?" Ms. Rapscott tried

to explain. "The *sponge* and the *frying pan*, both Take Matters into Their Own Hands . . . think about it."

The girls tried to look like they were thinking about it, but all Mildred could think was that neither the sponge nor the frying pan had hands to do anything with. But the more Mildred thought about it the more rattled she became, for she didn't like the idea of doing anything on her own—or without at least one corgi present. At least she had her distilled white vinegar, though. She felt in her skirt pocket for the jar to make sure that it was still there. It was. Annabelle could scoff all she wanted, but just this morning Mildred had placed a few drops of the stuff on each leg of her desk because it was wobbly, and it had worked like a charm—no more wobble. Nope, she wasn't going anywhere without her vinegar.

After lunch the girls filed into the classroom to see their backpacks lined up in a row. Would they be leaving for The Top today? Now?

"Birthday balloons out, class!" Ms. Rapscott ordered. "Please take notes as I explain How to Blow Up a Birthday Balloon!" Lewis demonstrated as the headmistress gave step-by-step instruction. When the balloon had reached the size of a large pumpkin, Ms. Rapscott finished by saying, "Tie the end in a double knot . . . tie the string to the end . . . and voilà! Birthday balloon!"

Bea waved her hand. "Ms. Rapscott! Ms. Rapscott, are we going to meet Fay at The Top tomorrow on Mildred's birthday?"

"That is up to you," Ms. Rapscott said mysteriously. Then she went to the window and looked through her binoculars.

The girls ran to the window chattering at once. "Do you see Fay? What's she doing? Is she having FUN? Is she riding Twinkle Toes? Is she on the Ferris wheel?"

Ms. Rapscott raised an eyebrow and pursed her lips but she wouldn't say. Instead she placed the binoculars on her desk. The girls had the awful feeling that their puzzling teacher had more questions than answers today. Every one of them was left wondering if they were meeting Fay at

The Top . . . and how were they supposed to get there on Mildred's birthday?

"Balloons!" Ms. Rapscott said. Clark handed her one. "It wouldn't be a birthday without balloons, class, so colorful, festive, and cheerful. But do not underestimate the common birthday balloon, because just like a true Rapscott Girl there is so much more to one than meets the eye."

Ms. Rapscott marched across the classroom, flung open the door, and released the balloon into the stormy sky. "You mark my words, that balloon will go far, girls—maybe even all the way to The Top!"

The girls watched the balloon rise and disappear up into the sky.

Chapter 13
Birthday Balloons

That night the sky was clear and there was only a whisper of wind. They were in between Hurricane Brunhilda and Bunny, causing a lull in the hurricanes that had pummeled them since their first day of school. As the girls changed into their pajamas they were all wondering about what the next day would bring. Would they set off to meet Fay? Would they finally earn the Great Rapscott Medal for Reaching The Top?

Bea climbed into her blue bed and could just see herself wearing the medal. *If I were Head Girl we'd be at The Top right now in our own pink and purple rooms with our own unicorn curled up by the fire,* Bea thought. She sat in her bed and stewed over the one person whose fault it would be if they didn't earn the medal tomorrow: Dahlia Thistle. Bea looked at the time. It was ten thirty. *Some Head Girl, she can't even remember that lights-out is at ten.*

Across the room Dahlia looked at the time and gasped. "Lights-out," Dahlia called in a small voice. She didn't sound like a Head Girl—not even to herself.

"Sweet dreams, Dahlia," Mildred said, even though she was too stirred up about her birthday to sleep.

"Sweet dreams," Dahlia replied softly. She covered up Harold and lay down, but she felt too unsettled to sleep as well.

"Good night," Annabelle said, but even she was wide awake. She had grown used to the sound of wind and rain lashing the dorm windows, and it was almost too quiet.

"You must not forget to grow," Ms. Rapscott reminded Dahlia every day. Dahlia had promised that she was trying and hoped that if she could just get a little bit bigger maybe Bea and

Annabelle would like her better. The only girl who had been a friend to her at Great Rapscott School was Mildred. Still, Dahlia never stopped thinking about her *real* friends—the boys at Mt. Everbest. There was her favorite, Reggie, who was so sensitive, and brave Ernest, and over-wrought Nathan, and Theodore who made terrible faces but was really a nice boy. There was poor Oscar who was always catching colds. She wondered how the new boys, Ricky and Nicky, were fitting in and if the others were still playing tricks on them. And what of Mr. Everbest, as busy as he was, going off with only one boot! Oh, how she wished she were back there where maybe she could help. How could anyone sleep with such worries?

Over in the blue bed Bea was still awake, too. "Do you think Fay is even *at* The Top anymore?" she said out loud so that everyone could hear.

"If she stops being happy she'll get kicked out, remember?" Mildred had been tossing and turning, trying to get comfortable, worried about how she would perform the next day. She just *had* to do better on her way up to The Top than she had done down at The Bottom.

"I hope we get there in time," Dahlia muttered. "I mean before Fay gets kicked out."

"Oh, we probably won't," Annabelle said breezily from her side of the room. "Fay's always doing something wrong."

Bea leaned up against the pillows with her chin to her chest and her forehead furrowed. *If only . . . if only . . .* Bea thought. *If only she could look through Ms. Rapscott's binoculars and see for herself.* Bea sat bolt upright. She swung her legs over the side of the bed, shoved her feet into her Rapscott boiled wool slippers and her arms into her Rapscott navy-blue-and-white quilted bathrobe, and hopped out of bed.

Annabelle sat up in bed. "Where are you going?"

But Bea was in too much of a hurry to answer. She scurried down the spiral stairs into the darkened classroom. She flicked on the lights and her

mouth dropped open. The room had been trans-
formed! The desks were covered in pink table-
cloths; the chairs had big green bows. There were
party hats and three brightly wrapped packages
on Ms. Rapscott's desk. Balloons were everywhere: tied to the stairs, the desks, and some
floated up at the ceiling. On the chalkboard had
been written: **HAPPY BIRTHDAY, MILDRED!**

"Wow," Bea said softly.

A moment later Mildred, Annabelle, and
Dahlia crept down the stairs and stood amazed
at their usually somber classroom.

"It's beautiful!" Mildred exclaimed.

"Shhhhh." Bea held a finger to her lips. The
clock on the wall said 10:41. They were supposed
to be in their beds asleep, not in the classroom.

Mildred went around the room touching everything and picked out a bunch of balloons that
spelled out the words: H A P P Y B I R T H D A Y.
She whirled around until she was dizzy.

Annabelle looked curiously at one of the packages on Ms. Rapscott's desk. It was wrapped in

pink paper and ribbon. She had never seen anything like it!

Dahlia's eyes were glued to the spiral stairs where she expected Ms. Rapscott to trot down any second. "We shouldn't be here right now," Dahlia said, but no one was listening. She spoke a little louder. "We have to go back to the dorm." Still no one answered her. Dahlia took a deep breath. "As Head Girl I demand you all go back upstairs!"

"Oh, hush up, before you wake the corgis," Bea hissed. "I'm just trying to make sure that Fay is still at The Top." She spied the binoculars right there on Ms. Rapscott's desk!

"But we have to go upstairs now!" Dahlia insisted.

"In a minute now—SHUUUSH," Bea said. She grabbed the binoculars and ran to the window to look but saw nothing. Without so much as a second thought she rushed to the classroom door that led outside. It was like the kind on a submarine and Bea twirled the handle to the left.

Dahlia frowned. She pointed her tiny finger at Bea and ordered, "Come away from that door this instant!"

Mildred stood motionless still holding her balloons. She didn't like the outdoors and liked it even less without Ms. Rapscott and at least one corgi. "Bea, do you think you should?"

"You always agree with everything Dahlia says," Bea snapped.

"I do not," Mildred said defensively.

"You do, too," Bea said, and gave the door one mighty tug. It popped open and made the same sound as if someone had pulled the seal off a giant vacuum-packed can of mixed nuts. *SHROOSH!*

Before Dahlia could voice her objections anymore, Bea went outside to get a better look. Stars twinkled above and there wasn't a cloud for miles. Bea searched the sky through the binoculars, turning in every direction. "I think I see her!"

Dahlia caught up. "Get inside!" she said as loud as she dared. "Come on—now!"

"Give it to me." Annabelle pulled at the binoculars to see for herself.

"Do you see Fay?" Mildred stood breathless with excitement. "Let *me* see!" She tried to get the binoculars away from Annabelle. "You're hogging them—and it's *my* birthday!"

"I'm still looking!" Annabelle elbowed Mildred away while Bea grabbed for the glasses, but Annabelle was tall and held them up in the air, too high for Bea to reach.

"Hold these a second, please?" Mildred handed the balloons to Dahlia, then she snatched the binoculars away from Annabelle. "It's *my* birthday; give them to *me*!" She looked and looked but didn't see anything. "I don't see her—but I see The Top! It's gold and sparkly and beautiful!"

"I want to see." Bea pushed Mildred and yanked the binoculars from her.

Suddenly there was a high-pitched call for help, and when they looked Dahlia was hanging at the end of several strands of balloons floating skyward.

"HELP!!!!!" she cried.

The girls looked at her with shock and then at one another.

"She's got your birthday balloons," Bea said incredulously. "Don't worry, Mildred! I'll get them back for you!" Bea yelled and raced inside the lighthouse. In a flash she was back outside with as many balloons as it took to rise into the sky.

"Help!" Dahlia shouted again. Her voice sounded very far away.

"Hang on, Dahlia!" Mildred screamed, and ran to get her own bunch of balloons. "Wait up, Bea!" she called.

Annabelle shook her head and exhaled loudly through her teeth. She knew she was the only one of this lot who could make sure that nobody got squashed on the ground. She gathered balloon after balloon until her feet also lifted off the ground, floated out of the door, and flew off into the night.

Chapter 14
Dahlia Goes Far

on't let go . . . don't let go . . . don't let go . . .
Dahlia repeated this over and over to herself
as she rose higher and higher till she was higher
than even the lighthouse. She didn't dare let go—
Mildred would never forgive her for losing her
birthday balloons. The wind caught the balloons,
and she was borne on the breeze that took her
over the sandy road along the cliffs where a soli-
tary jogger called up to her, "Going far, I see!"

"Yes, thank you!" Dahlia called back because
even though she was terrified she remembered
from her first day of school when Ms. Rapscott
had said, "A Rapscott Girl must always be polite."

Over the trees she floated. Her Rapscott slippers dangled out from beneath her heavy quilted

bathrobe. She held on with all her might, traveling farther and farther away. With each blink the light from the lighthouse became dimmer and dimmer. Dahlia flew out of town and passed over a woman below who was pulling a wagon full of pumpkins. There was a parrot on the woman's shoulder that squawked, "HEY HO!" The woman called, "Taking matters into your own hands, I see!"

"Y-Yes!" Dahlia stammered, as it was difficult to talk and hang on to balloons at the same time.

The lighthouse blinked out of sight and Dahlia floated on. There were no people here, and just a few porch lights burned from houses that became few and far between. Dahlia was not so high that she couldn't see a fox make its way across an open field and an owl swoop through some trees. Several bats flapped past her, popping one of the balloons. Dahlia sank lower in the sky and realized that all she had to do was let go of one balloon at a time and she would drift safely to the ground. But then what of poor Mildred? She'd never had birthday balloons in her entire life! Dahlia hung on until she could figure out what to do. Then off in the distance she heard something. Was it music?

Far behind, Bea, Mildred, and Annabelle were a sight to see floating in the night sky at the ends of birthday balloons. They flew right over the yolky glow of streetlamps. They passed over rooftops on their way out of town, and on his way into a doughnut shop a policeman called up to them, "Good luck on your way to The Top!" Mildred was far too preoccupied to answer back. Her feet were well over the tree-tops. The air was chilled and she was glad for her quilted robe. She also never dared take her eyes off Dahlia up ahead.

The girls floated farther and farther. The air was still and the sky was filled with stars that twinkled down on them, and there was the distinct sound of music that was nothing like Bea had ever heard. Of course she'd never been on a merry-go-round or to a skating rink because her parents were too busy—but if she had Bea would have recognized the music at once.

Suddenly a shimmering building came into view and Bea was dazzled. Light blazed from long narrow windows. Tall towers soared and were crowned with golden balustrades.

Annabelle saw it, too. It glowed deliciously off in the distance. Though she'd never told the other girls (because she knew they would tease her) she'd always wanted to go to this thing called a dinner party! She'd read about them in the *Encyclopedia Britannica*. Dinner parties were very adult, and very civilized, where people gathered to eat only the best food, had only the best conversation, and where you were expected to have only the best manners. Surely the best place in the world would have dinner parties every night! She held on even harder to her balloons in the hope that they would take her all the way to The Top.

Mildred bobbed in the night sky spellbound by the beauty of The Top. It glowed like a birthday candle—*her* birthday candle. For a moment she forgot all about Dahlia and wished with all her heart to get to The Top and see the candy tree that Fay had said was growing in the lobby.

"Look!" Bea shouted. The music was clearly coming from a Ferris wheel that was on the highest part of the building, and at the very top of it there was a girl! "FAY! FAY!" Bea screamed. "It's us!"

But when Mildred turned her attention back to Dahlia, the girl was letting go of her birthday balloons. One at a time they flew away. Down, down, down Dahlia drifted. "We're coming, Dahlia!" Mildred hollered, and when she reached the area where she thought the small girl had landed, Mildred, too, let go of her birthday balloons one at a time.

"What are you doing?" Bea yelled out incredulously. "We're almost at The Top!"

"We can't leave Dahlia here all by herself!" Mildred cried. "We just can't!" A minute later she landed with a *THUMP!* in the dirt.

Bea let go of one balloon after another, too. She sighed. If Mildred couldn't leave Dahlia then she certainly couldn't leave Mildred—but Bea wasn't happy about it. *THUMP!* She landed in the dirt, too.

Annabelle reluctantly let go of her balloons. *THUMP!* She landed as well.

What a disappointment. They weren't at the wonder-filled place with the Ferris wheel, the candy tree, unicorns, and dinner parties every night. Instead they stood in the middle of a cornfield, in the middle of nowhere, in the middle of the night. A wolf howled in the distance. A cold wind blew, and they pulled the collars of their robes around their necks.

"I'm sorry," Dahlia called to Mildred as soon as they were within earshot. All except Dahlia had forgotten to hang on to at least one balloon—including Mildred. Dahlia handed Mildred the only one left. "It's all I could save," she said sadly.

"My birthday balloon!" Mildred thanked Dahlia, happy to have at least one.

Seeing this, Bea could have kicked herself for

not thinking to save a balloon. Never did she want to pinch someone really hard more than she did Dahlia Thistle right then. Bea balled up her fists, screwed up her face, and yelled, "OH! Why did you come down *here*?"

Without answering, Dahlia took off at a trot toward the edge of the cornfield.

"A box?" Bea exclaimed angrily when she got closer. "We gave up going to The Top to meet Fay for a box?"

"Ugh!" Annabelle pressed her lips together in disapproval. "It's a Mt. Everbest box!"

It sat quietly with no signs of life. Dahlia crept up to it.

"Hello?" she called softly, but there was no reply. "Hello?" It seemed as though no one was in the box until there was a bloodcurdling yell: "FERRET FACE!"

Bea, Mildred, and Annabelle leaped back and dashed away as far as they could.

"Let go of my foot you stupid—" someone said. The box tipped, and cardboard bulged in places as if it was being pummeled with kicks from the inside.

"You're an idiot!"

"No, you are!" Then the box tumbled on its side and two boys spilled out. They stopped arguing with each other, and their eyes grew wide as if they'd just seen a ghost. "Dahlia!"

"Ricky! Nicky!" Dahlia yelled with delight. She would never forget how the twins had stood up to the girls for her down at The Bottom.

Right away the twins eyed the other girls suspiciously. "Are they being nice to you?" Ricky asked.

"'Cause if they're not," Nicky piped up, "we'll squash them like bugs!" Then he ground his heel in the dirt to demonstrate.

A smile tugged at Dahlia's lips, but she didn't want any more trouble. "The girls are being very nice to me now," she fibbed.

Annabelle could see this was getting them nowhere. She elbowed her way in front of Dahlia to find out what these two horrible boys from

Mt. Everbest were up to. "I demand to know what you are doing here in the middle of this cornfield!"

"What's it to you?" Ricky snarled. "Yeah, four-eyes!" Nicky added, and the two boys snickered at the bespectacled girl.

"Oh, you . . . you . . . *boy*!" Annabelle quickly took off the belt from her bathrobe and proceeded to wrap it around Ricky's wrists. "I'm placing you under arrest!"

"I demand you don't!" Dahlia said, using her best Head Girl voice. "They'll be good—won't you, boys?"

"No," they both said at the same time.

Annabelle asked Bea for help, and she happily took her belt and wrapped it around Nicky's wrists. Then she gave it a hard tug.

"OW!" Nicky cried. "What am I under arrest for?" Both boys were a mess. Their curly dark hair was matted to their heads, and they had cracker crumbs and cheese bits ground into the front of their Everbest blazers.

"For being a revolting boy," Annabelle said. "Plus you smell and your uniforms are crusty with food!"

Ricky laughed in her face. "At least we're not wearing pajamas!"

"You leave our pajamas out of this!" Annabelle said sharply.

Dahlia tried to calm everyone down. "What are you boys doing out here all by yourselves?" she asked gently.

"We ran away." The boys looked down. "Just took our box and left."

Dahlia was perplexed. It was an oversized box made specifically to ship two. "But however did you carry it all the way from Mt. Everbest?"

"I attached those." Ricky pointed with both hands, since they were still tied up. "To make rope handles."

Nicky explained, "Then I tied these ropes to the handles and we just pulled." He sounded proud of his handiwork. "It's a good box, too. Keeps us warm and dry at night, and we've got plenty of snacks to last us."

"You have snacks to last you till when?" Bea narrowed her eyes and gave the cord that was around his wrists a yank.

Nicky yelped.

"You're on your way to The Top, aren't you?" Bea interrogated the boy. "You think you can beat us there, don't you?"

"Admit it!" Annabelle shouted.

"And what if we do?" Nicky barked, but he looked like he might cry.

"But didn't Mr. Everbest come to find you?" Dahlia asked.

"Ever since we got to school Mr. Everbest has been busy." Ricky sighed.

"It's been awful," Nicky added.

"Awful, how?" Bea asked sharply.

Nicky sniffed. "When the other boys aren't ignoring us they sit on our heads and put mayonnaise in our shoes."

Ricky continued. "All we get is microwave popcorn for breakfast, and there's no time to read us a story or make us go to bed at night, no one to teach us important things like How to

Knit a Scarf or whether or not to refrigerate jars of things after they've been opened. And we're always getting lost because the headmaster is too busy to teach us How to Find Your Way."

The girls exchanged knowing looks.

"Disgraceful!" Annabelle huffed. "Why, you might as well be at home."

Ricky stuck out his lower lip defiantly. "We're going all the way to The Top all by ourselves!"

"Yeah, that's what you think," Bea said.

"Oh yeah?" Nicky challenged her.

No way was Bea letting two stupid boys get there before her. She stuck her face in his. "Yeah."

Both boys sat down hard in the dirt. They knew Bea was right. They weren't going anywhere—not with their wrists tied up.

One by one the girls sat down hard in the dirt, too, their chins in their hands, all equally unhappy for different reasons. Bea hadn't gotten to The Top. Mildred didn't want to spend her birthday in a cornfield. Annabelle wouldn't be dining at any dinner parties, and she did not approve of children sitting in the dirt in the middle of the night, completely unsupervised. Dahlia felt bad that she hadn't been able to help Ricky and Nicky more and, after hearing how things were at Mt. Everbest, she was more worried than ever for her friends.

Chapter 15
A BRILLIANT IDEA

The four girls sat wondering the same thing: How were they ever going to get back to Great Rapscott School?

"Maybe if I shout really loud—louder than I've ever shouted in my entire life—Ms. Rapscott will hear," Bea suggested.

"We're so far away, though," Mildred groaned.

"But if anyone can be heard it's Bea," Annabelle said.

Bea took a deep breath, and Mildred, Annabelle, and Dahlia put their hands over their ears. Then Bea screamed at the top of her lungs, **"MS. RAPSCOTT!! HELP!"**

She stopped and they all listened.

They waited. Except for the breeze that rattled

the dried-out leaves of the cornstalks all was silent.

"I know!" Bea said next. "I'll try calling for Lewis and Clark!" She cupped her hands around her mouth and screeched even louder this time. *"LEWIS! CLARK! HE-E-E-E-ELP! HELP!! HELP!!! HELP!!!!"*

She stopped and they all listened.

They waited again, but neither Ms. Rapscott nor Lewis and Clark came to the girls' rescue.

"Too bad we got rid of all those balloons," Bea muttered.

"We have one left," Mildred said brightly.

Annabelle was less than enthusiastic. "A whole lot of good that'll do us."

Mildred had to agree. She sighed. "What good is one balloon?"

"Unless . . ." Dahlia laughed. "It was one *big* balloon."

Suddenly Mildred's cheeks turned a beautiful rosy pink. "I just got the most brilliant idea for how to get us out of here!" Mildred seemed to light up from within, which is how it is with brilliant ideas. "I'll blow up this little balloon into a great big one!" she exclaimed.

"That's your brilliant idea?" Annabelle rolled her eyes and so did Bea.

Mildred was disappointed at her classmates' lack of enthusiasm. "It's a brilliant idea—what's the problem?"

"The balloon will pop before it ever gets that big, Mildred." Annabelle shook her head. "That's the problem!"

Mildred smiled slyly. She reached into the pocket of her bathrobe, and her fingers closed over the jar that she always brought with her wherever she went. She held it up for everyone to see, and it twinkled magically in the starlight. "Distilled white vinegar from Ms. Rapscott . . . solves any problem—remember?" With that she quickly untied the remaining birthday balloon and let out all the air. She dipped it in the vinegar. Then she began to blow while her skeptical Rapscott classmates and two dubious Everbest Boys looked on.

Mildred blew, and blew, and with every breath

the balloon got bigger and bigger. When it was as large as the box, Mildred began to be lifted off the ground and Dahlia had to grab her by her feet to keep her from floating away. Mildred continued to blow.

Bea sprang into action. She climbed into the box and gathered the ropes that Ricky and Nicky had installed to pull it there. The balloon was soon the size of an elephant, and Mildred continued to blow. Dahlia was ascending into the air as well, and Annabelle caught her by the feet before the two girls and the balloon could float away. Then Bea grabbed Annabelle's feet as she, too, was lifted off the ground.

"Quick! Get in the box!" Bea ordered the boys.

The box skipped along the ground, pulled by the balloon which was now the size of a dinosaur. Ricky made a run for it, scrambled inside, and pulled in his twin even though he wouldn't stop calling him ferret face. Both boys were secretly happy, as they were tired of being lost all the time with just each other.

Mildred had stopped blowing. She tied the end in a double knot just like Ms. Rapscott had shown them. Then Bea reeled in Annabelle, Dahlia, and Mildred, who all worked quickly to tie the ropes from the box to the end of the balloon.

By now they were airborne, soaring through the sky. Huge thunderheads had formed heralding a new storm. They were blown by the winds of Hurricane Bunny on her way to Great Rapscott School. Nicky called Bea "Pee," and she refused to untie both boys' hands. The girls watched intently for their school to come into view and were relieved to see the familiar blinking light after a few minutes.

There were Lewis and Clark and Ms. Rapscott. They stood on top of the lighthouse and leaned over the railing to catch the balloon as it floated by. They held it steady as the girls and the twins climbed out.

Lewis checked his watch and nodded. It was 12:01.

"Perfect timing!" Ms. Rapscott exclaimed. She

made a little hop for joy and trilled. "It's officially your birthday, Mildred. Do you feel any older?"

Mildred wasn't sure how old she was in the first place, so it was hard for her to tell if she felt any older. "Older than what?" Mildred asked.

"Older than eight," Ms. Raspcott replied.

"You mean I'm nine?" Mildred asked.

"Correct!" Ms. Rapscott said. "Congratulations! It's quite an accomplishment for a girl like you, Mildred!"

Annabelle pushed Ricky, and Bea shoved Nicky in front of the headmistress. "We found *them*," both girls said.

Ms. Raspcott was genuinely happy to see the boys.

"They've got me and Nicky under arrest, Ms. Rapscott," Ricky complained, and showed the headmistress his wrists that were still tied.

"I'm sure for good reason. A Rapscott Girl is always just, Ricky—never forget that," Ms. Rapscott replied curtly. Lewis raised an eyebrow. Clark gave both boys a dirty look and made a notation on his clipboard.

"But, Ms. Rapscott," Nicky cried, "they said I was under arrest because I was a revolting boy!"

Ms. Rapscott tilted her head in thought. "In all fairness, girls, Ricky and Nicky can't really help that. . . ."

Bea pushed her way in front of the headmistress to explain. "He was trying to get to The Top before us!"

"To get to The Top before you?" Ms. Rapscott slapped her leg. "So that's it!" She waved a hand. Clark furiously erased something on his clipboard, and Lewis untied both boys' wrists. "They are innocent, girls!" she proclaimed. "You are free, boys—and no longer under arrest!"

"But why not?" Annabelle asked indignantly.

"Because Ricky and Nicky were just Taking Matters into Their Own Hands, Annabelle." Ms. Rapscott beamed. "I am pleased to say it's a worthy lesson that you all have learned tonight, class." Then she put one arm around both boys' shoulders and ushered them inside the lighthouse. "I'm sure Mr. Everbest is looking all over for you two."

"He's busy now, Ms. Rapscott," Ricky muttered. "I doubt he's noticed."

"Never mind. You must pull up your socks," Ms. Rapscott said with conviction. "And stand up straight, Nicky, an Everbest Boy does not slouch."

The two corgis hauled the Mt. Everbest box over the railing. They let the air out of the balloon, which returned to its original size, and presented it to Mildred so that she would never forget this birthday.

By then it was quite late and the bad weather from Bunny had scampered in. The girls were sent off to bed. Ms. Rapscott and the corgis packed the twins in their box with a warm quilt—because the temperature had dropped dramatically. The boys were also given a large slice of Mildred's birthday cake, and the box was set outside in a **WIDE OPEN AREA** to be sent to Mt. Everbest Academy.

Back in the dorm the girls were in their beds, but Annabelle couldn't stop thinking about Mildred's brilliant idea. It just didn't make sense that distilled white vinegar could have such an enormous effect on such a little balloon. Annabelle asked Mildred if she could see that jar of vinegar for a clue or indication of magic. Annabelle sniffed it, she dipped the tip of her pinkie in and tasted it. She held the jar up to the light. After all that, the distilled white vinegar seemed entirely unremarkable in every way.

Even so, from that day on Annabelle never went anywhere without some.

Chapter 16

A Great Rapscott Birthday

The girls woke to a cold, dark morning, grim with rain and thunder. Hurricane Bunny was a quick storm and had blown out to sea just in time for another hurricane to take her place. Hurricane Buster was Known for Huge Frothy White Waves. When Bea threw back the covers on her bed and ran to look out the window, sure enough waves were breaking all the way up the lighthouse practically to their dorm.

Bea jumped back into bed to warm her freezing toes. "Mildred, are you awake?" she called over to the next bed. Ever since the night of the bad hurricane when Dahlia Thistle had been thrown from her bed Mildred had been best friends with her. But Bea hoped that maybe since she'd tried to save Mildred's birthday balloons, Mildred would like her again. Then Bea remembered she'd let all the balloons go—it'd been Dahlia who had thought to hold on to one.

Mildred peeked her head out from behind the bed curtain, her hair a mass of red curls. She'd been awake for the past hour waiting for her birthday to start. "What, Bea?"

"Forget it," Bea mumbled.

Just then Ms. Raspcott came skipping down the spiral stairs, and Lewis and Clark came up from below with trays of hot chocolate to serve the girls in their beds.

"What a glorious day for a birthday celebration!" Ms. Rapscott exclaimed. She threw open the window and inhaled deeply as if it were a beautiful summer day with birds singing and the sun shining. The headmistress leaned out the window so far that her feet left the ground. Lewis and Clark held on to her fisherman's sweater to keep her from falling. When they pulled her inside she was dripping wet and in one hand was a glass bottle with a cork stopper. "Look, girls! There's a message inside!" The corgis pricked up their ears with interest. The girls could see a piece of rolled-up paper, and when Ms. Rapscott slid it out she made a little hop for joy. "It's another Friendly Letter from Fay!" The girls scrambled out of bed and all started to talk at once.

Bea barraged the headmistress with questions. "Did she see us from the Ferris wheel? Did she finally do something wrong? Is she unhappy yet?" She asked hopefully because though she liked her classmate it was hard to hear about someone else having that much fun.

"Let's see!" Ms. Rapscott said, and began to read:

Dear Ms. ~~Rapsot Dripstart Rimsuit~~ Rapscot
and ~~Bee, Be, BAe~~ classmates,

I got your letter. Thanks!

I'm still at The Top! Everything is wonderfle!

I had hot dogs, spagetti and chocolate ~~mild~~ milc for breckfas. Twinkle Toes is better than ever and says HI!

I'm learning so much herre! There's this thing called a **DINNER PARTY**.

Annabelle interrupted. "I knew it!"

Ms. Rapscott held up a hand for quiet and continued.

Every night they have a **DINNER PARTY** in an all gold ballroom! People stand around with little plates of PARTY FOOD: things like pickles on crackers and avocadoe dips but my favorite are **PIGS IN A BLANKET**.

This time Mildred interrupted. "Pigs in a blanket?"

Ms. Rapscott held up a hand again and continued reading.

—their not real pigs!!!! They're little hot dogs wrapped in pie crust. Theres also a lot a **CHANDELEERS**—those are lights that hang down from the gold ceiling made of diamons. Last night I went to the **DINNER PARTY** dressed as Ms. ~~Rastot Rappspot~~ RAPPSCOT!!!!! I had on a fisherman's sweater and brown pants and boots and everything!!! I got a STANDING OVATION— that's when everyone stands and claps and whisssles at you for being wonderfle. I got my picture taken a lot. Someone even wrote a song all about me called: "Fay."

So as you can see I am still happy! But when are you coming to meet me here? I ride the ferus wheel every night searching the sky in case you and the girls happen to blow by on the wind. I can't wait to see everyone again. There's still no kids here. I jus hope I can stay happy until you get here . . . please hurry.

Your student and classmate,

Fay

In spite of all the errors Ms. Rapscott seemed pleased with Fay's note. "Shall we write back, class?" The girls all agreed they should, and Clark readied himself with his pen and wrote while Ms. Rapscott dictated:

Howdy, Fay!

Congrats for staying at The Top!
We do hope you are still enjoying this wonderful hurricane season! Today we are going to learn How to Celebrate a Birthday. It so happens to be Mildred's and we wish you were here.
Never fear! We will meet you soon. We have just a few more things to learn and then we will be heading straight to The Top!

Warm regards to Twinkle Toes.

Yours truly,
Ms. Rapscott

"Sign your names, girls!" Ms. Rapscott sent the Friendly Letter around the room. She then rolled it up, put it back in the glass bottle, sealed it with the cork, opened the window, and a wave licked it from her hand. Ms. Rapscott made her way to the spiral stairs with the corgis right behind her.

The girls hurried to get ready for Morning Meeting. Mildred was the first one dressed. "Wow!" she said as she waited for the others. "Fay sure sounds happy."

Bea expertly tied the neckerchief on her uniform in a square knot, "I don't think Fay's all that happy." She adjusted her hat. "I think Fay is lonely," Bea said. "She'll be back here in a week!"

"At least those awful Everbest Boys haven't gotten there yet," Annabelle said, and Bea wholeheartedly agreed because it was her worst fear.

At Morning Meeting Ms. Rapscott's voice rang throughout the lighthouse. "Everyone say 'Happy Birthday' to Mildred, class," she instructed because none of the girls knew that it was customary to do so.

Then Ms. Rapscott asked, "Does anyone know How to Celebrate a Birthday?"

None of the girls did since their parents had all been too busy for that.

Ms. Rapscott took from her desk the little box that was wrapped in pink paper. It had the words "Happy Birthday" written in lime green all over it, was tied with a bright pink ribbon, and there was a little yellow envelope tucked under a bow. "*This* is a birthday present, girls." She turned it 360 degrees so that they could see it from every angle.

Dahlia raised her hand. "I think I got a birthday present once."

Ms. Raspcott smiled. "Do tell, Dahlia."

Bea and Annabelle rolled their eyes.

Dahlia stood. "One day my grandmother's mailman found me at the post office? Because my grandmother forgot me there when she got busy? So they took me to the police station and gave me a grape lollipop? Is that . . . a birthday present?"

Ms. Rapscott touched the side of her nose with her index finger. "Did it come with a card, Dahlia?"

"I don't think so." Dahlia sat down a little embarrassed.

Annabelle huffed and Bea snickered.

Ms. Rapscott waved a hand, "Then it's a present, Dahlia, but not a birthday present."

The headmistress pointed to the little yellow envelope. "*This* is called a birthday card, girls." She held up the card, and it had Mildred's name written on it in glitter.

The girls all strained forward in their seats to look in amazement.

"But why is there a card *and* a present?" Annabelle wanted to know. It seemed a bit excessive to her.

"A birthday card tells who the birthday present is from, Annabelle," Ms. Rapscott replied. "Furthermore you cannot give a birthday present without a card, but you may give a birthday card without a present." It seemed very complicated this business of birthday presents and cards. The girls wrote it all down. "And . . ." Ms. Rapscott finished, "the most important thing of all to remember is that one must *always* be surprised on one's birthday!"

Then Ms. Rapscott handed Mildred the first of the three birthday presents. The red-haired girl began to open it with her classmates looking on.

"Wait!" Ms. Rapscott stopped her. "One usually opens the card first, Mildred." Lewis and Clark nodded that it was so.

Mildred slid the yellow envelope out from under the bow and opened it.

"Read it out loud for all of us to hear," Ms. Rapsott said merrily.

Mildred read:

A Rapscott birthday is always Great
with presents, ice cream, and a cake.
But, dear Mildred, be advised
it's not a birthday without
a Great Rapscott surprise!

Happy Birthday!

Yours truly,
Ms. Rapscott and Lewis and Clark

The girls exchanged glances, a little unsure about what the poem meant by "a Great Rapscott surprise." With Ms. Rapscott it could mean almost anything. But Mildred for once was too excited to worry. "Can I open it now?" she asked. Ms. Rapscott nodded that she could.

"A rock!" Mildred took it gently from the box like it might break. It was smooth and fit perfectly in the palm of her hand. No one had given her a rock before or anything else for that matter.

"Not just any rock," Ms. Rapscott said. "This is a Rapscott rock."

"What does it do?" Annabelle asked skeptically.

"Absolutely nothing, Annabelle," Ms. Rapscott replied. "And yet observe the rock . . . steady . . . constant . . . strong. We could do worse than to try to be just like this rock!"

Next Mildred opened Clark's present. "Wow!" she said even more surprised.

"An old ball?" Annabelle said.

"Not just any old ball," Ms. Raspcott corrected. "Clark's favorite ball that he's had since he was a small corgi—and it still has plenty of bounce—just like a Rapscott Girl. Say thank you, Mildred."

Mildred thanked the corgi and said, "I'll treasure it always."

The last present was from Ms. Rapscott, who had to tell the girl what the present was. "Earmuffs." She put them on Mildred to demonstrate how they worked.

Mildred felt the fuzzy material that hugged her ears. "Should I be like earmuffs?" she said a little loudly because now she couldn't hear with them on.

"Be like earmuffs, Mildred?" Ms. Rapscott said indignantly, and Mildred was surprised to hear the headmistress say, "Of course not! Don't be ridiculous! But you will be happy for those earmuffs when winter comes next semester during blizzard season."

If blizzard season was anything like hurricane season Mildred could see where earmuffs might come in handy at Great Rapscott School.

Now it's your turn, girls," Ms. Rapscott said. "You have the rest of the day to find a present or to make a card for Mildred."

The girls pulled their desks together, and Mildred had to stay on the other side of the room while they discussed what their birthday present to her would be.

Bea looked at the pencil in her hand. "How about a pencil?"

"She's already got one of those," Dahlia said.

"Or some shells?" Annabelle said.

"What's she going to do with shells?" Bea asked.

"Make a shell collection—what do you think?" Annabelle said impatiently. "I mean, if we give her a pencil what's to stop us from giving her toothpaste, or a fork?"

"But if we give her shells," Bea reasoned, "we might as well give her a cantaloupe or an asparagus."

Annabelle shook her head vigorously. "You're missing the point!"

Bea knew the point was that Annabelle

wanted to be the one to suggest the present. "So what's Mildred supposed to do with a shell collection?"

Annabelle shrugged. "Collect more shells."

"Big deal," Bea muttered. "Don't give me shells on my birthday—okay?"

"I wouldn't dream of it." Annabelle poked her nose in the air. "I've already decided to give you a pencil."

"This is getting us nowhere," Dahlia interjected. "I think we should just make her a card."

"I heard that!" Mildred called from the other side of the room.

All three girls threw up their hands in frustration because now it wouldn't be a surprise—which seemed to be an important criterion for a present.

"Girls!" Ms. Rapscott stood over them. "Have you decided on a present or a card for Mildred?"

"No, Ms. Rapscott." They sat utterly flummoxed about what to give Mildred. After lunch they tried again to come up with an idea. They talked and talked and argued some more. They stuffed

Mildred's ears with cotton because she kept trying to hear and ruin the surprise. Halfway through the afternoon Ms. Rapscott asked again, "Have you thought of what to give Mildred yet?"

"No, Ms. Rapscott," they all said glumly.

Lewis pointed to his watch.

"You must have something before the day is through!" Ms. Rapscott abruptly turned on her heel and announced that she and the corgis were going to town for an hour. There would be no help coming from her. And so the girls listened to the loud, *ticktock*, *ticktock*, of the clock, wondering what on earth to give to Mildred on her birthday.

Suddenly Bea had a strange gleam in her eyes. "You know what would *really* be a surprise?"

"What?" Dahlia and Annabelle both said.

"What if we took Mildred to the seventh floor?" Bea whispered.

"It's off-limits," Dahlia was quick to remind them—as if Bea didn't already know that.

"But this is Mildred's birthday!" Bea said in a low voice. "Like the card said: *It's not a birthday without a Great Rapscott surprise.* What could be a better surprise?"

Before anyone could object further Bea called to Mildred, "We have the perfect thing for your birthday—but we need to blindfold you." Bea already had her neckerchief off and was tying it over the red-haired girl's eyes. She took Mildred by the hand and led her up the stairs. "This is going to be the best birthday present ever!"

"I can't wait!" Mildred said.

They climbed past the kitchen, the bathroom, the dorm, Ms. Rapscott's bedroom, and the pajama room. But just as they reached the stairway to the seventh floor, Mildred balked. She'd been counting floors by each turn of the stairs. Her face went white and she stammered, "I-Is th-th-this the seventh f-floor?"

Bea stood below the hatch which was closed. Just as she started to push it open the lights went out. The girls screamed, and there was an ear-piercing siren, **"BERRR-RUP!! BEEEEER-UP! BEEERRRR-UP!"**

Mildred tore off the blindfold and she, Bea, Annabelle, and Dahlia raced back down the stairs, their feet barely touching the steps. Mildred stumbled to her desk clutching her heart. Just as she collapsed into her chair the siren stopped.

Ms. Rapscott entered the room. She tapped her toe and looked very stern. "It's almost the end of the day, girls," she said crossly. "I do hope you have thought up an appropriate present for Mildred?"

Annabelle and Dahlia were silent and shoved Bea forward. She stood looking extremely remorseful and guilty. Mildred sat gasping for breath and finally uttered, "What a surprise."

"I can see that, Mildred," Ms. Rapscott said pleased. "It's not a birthday without one! Very good, class!" Then the headmistress made a surprising announcement that in honor of Mildred's birthday the girls would be allowed to take the rest of the day to Have a Lot of Fun.

There was a definite twinkle in Ms. Rapscott's eye as she took them all for a bracing walk along the cliffs. They watched Hurricane Buster blow out to sea and Hurricane Charlotte, who was Known for Having Hail That Tasted Like Buttered Popcorn, arrive, and it was the most surprising, happiest birthday that Mildred ever had.

Chapter 17

A Good Day for Things to Go Badly

For the next three weeks Ms. Rapscott's girls were put through their paces like never before. On any given day Bea could be practicing how to climb a tree while Mildred, Annabelle, and Dahlia could be studying the best way to build a fort. On one particularly dark afternoon Lewis and Clark gave the girls a lesson in How to Toast a Marshmallow. It was surprising how much they had to learn. Bea had never heard of waffles, Mildred had never heard of dodgeball, Annabelle origami, and Dahlia jelly beans.

All the while the days were getting shorter and the nights longer. The hurricanes blew in and out with so much frequency, it was hard to keep track of which hurricane was which. But the storms never stopped Ms. Rapscott from taking the girls into town for various errands. She walked ahead with her back ramrod straight, her large nose tilted skyward, and Lewis and Clark at her side with the girls following behind in single file. They carried their notebooks along to write down anything just in case Ms. Rapscott had something important to say.

Of course Ms. Rapscott *always* had something important to say.

On one of their trips, when they passed a store she stopped to look in the window at a set of marshmallow-toasting forks. She immediately sent the corgis in to buy them and said, "Remember, girls, whenever you buy something always make sure that it is something you like."

On their way home they passed a man selling saxophones. "Saxophones! Saxophones, for sale!" he called. "Saxophone, Ms. Rapscott?"

"No, thank you," she replied, and when they

were far enough away so that the man couldn't hear she said, "But remember, girls, never buy anything that you don't like just because you don't want to give someone Hurt Feelings."

Bea glanced back.

"Saxophone?" the man said a little sadly.

Ms. Rapscott paid no attention, "He'll get over it, Bea." She strode along. "Who can think of some other examples of why anyone would buy something that they don't like?"

"Because they're busy?" Mildred offered.

Annabelle added, "Or because everyone else is buying it—?"

"—and they don't want to feel left out?" Dahlia said.

"Precisely, girls," Ms. Rapscott replied.

They often went to lunch at the Big White Lighthouse Luncheonette, where they learned How to Order from a Menu. "Never order the same thing twice, Annabelle," Ms. Rapscott warned the girl because Being Old for Her Age had made her set in her ways. "It shows a lack of imagination. A Rapscott Girl is always imaginative."

At these lunches they had discussions about Going Far. So over grilled cheese and root beer one afternoon, Annabelle asked, "Are there any Dinner Party Dos and Don'ts, Ms. Rapscott?"

"Oh yes," Ms. Rapscott said. "Always keep your forehead off the table, never eat your soup with your salad fork, and never, ever, say the words 'pickled peppers' with your mouth full."

Annabelle didn't think she'd ever be inclined to do any of those things anyway and was certain there had to be more to know.

"Indeed, there is much more to know," Ms. Raspcott continued. "You will need to engage in interesting conversation, Annabelle—remember a Rapscott Girl is never dull."

"But what sorts of things are dull?" Annabelle wasn't sure at all and neither were the other girls.

"There are some subjects that are best to avoid, class," Ms. Rapscott warned. "For instance, shower curtains, lightbulbs, and knee socks—terribly boring. And never launch into a monologue about fertilizer, extension cords, or ironing boards."

"But, Ms. Rapscott, those are the Don'ts but what about the Dos?" Annabelle asked.

"Ah, the Dos." Ms. Rapscott smiled because the Dos were just as important as the Don'ts. "My rule of thumb is to always talk about things that make me wonder."

Mildred looked up from where she was blowing bubbles through her straw into her root beer. "Things that make you wonder?"

"Exactly, Mildred," Ms. Rapscott said. "For instance haven't you ever wondered why you can't eat grass?"

Mildred hadn't ever thought about it but now that she had, she wondered, "I can't eat grass?"

"No, Mildred," Ms. Rapscott said, "you can't eat grass."

The girls sat quietly because now they were wondering, too, why they couldn't eat grass.

"And then there is the common housefly," Ms. Rapscott continued. "They only have a life span of about one month. I've often wondered, do they have a different sense of time? Is one second to a housefly like one month to us? And is that why it's so hard to catch one?"

None of the girls knew, and now they were wondering, too.

Ms. Rapscott motioned for the check because lunch was almost over. "I continue to wonder, is macaroni art really art? Can you freeze cheese? Is it best to sleep on your back?" Lewis and Clark paid the bill, and the headmistress stood to put on her bonnet. The corgis gave the thumbs-up, and Ms. Rapscott sailed out of the luncheonette. "Always remember to wonder, girls, and you will never be dull!"

It was toward the end of their sixth week of the fall semester and well into October that the light-house stood spookily in the mournful gray light. The sea was restless and the wind moaned. It was a good day for things to go badly.

Ms. Rapscott stood before the girls, their pencils poised. "You should be aware that girls of busy parents have 83.8 percent more bad days than good ones. So, it is important that you learn How to Make a Bad Day Good." Ms. Rapscott loved having a bad day because it gave her a chance to turn it into a good one.

Lewis looked up from the window where he was watching Hurricane Cordelia roll in, Known for Having the Wettest Rain. The corgi nodded to Ms. Rapscott. Clark stood by the chalkboard and wrote: **HOW TO MAKE A BAD DAY GOOD**.

Ms. Rapscott continued. "In order to learn How to Make a Bad Day Good, we must first have a bad day, class."

Clark wrote: **HOW TO MAKE YOUR DAY GO BADLY.**

The girls sat at attention with their pencils poised ready to write.

"STEP ONE!" Ms. Rapscott announced. "Put a pebble in your shoe." In her hand between her thumb and forefinger was a pea-sized pebble. "A pebble in the shoe is one of the best ways to have a bad day, girls." Ms. Rapscott took off her boot and was about to drop the pebble in it.

Bea called out, "Don't do it—it's going to hurt!"

"Of course it's going to hurt, Bea—how else do you expect me to have a bad day?" With that she dropped the pebble in her boot and slipped it on. "See?" The girls held their breath as Ms. Rapscott paced in front of them. "Ow . . . ow . . . ow . . ." she said. "This is definitely starting to make my day worse—but class, a pebble in the shoe is not nearly enough to cause a really bad day . . . ow."

Clark wrote: **STEP TWO.**

Ms. Rapscott held up one finger. "To truly have a bad day you must tell yourself, 'It could be better,' whenever anything good happens."

Just then a red postman's truck zoomed up in front of the lighthouse. Ms. Rapscott ran to the door. "Ow . . . ow . . . ow."

"Congratulations, Ms. Rapscott." The postman handed her a large bird feeder. "You won!"

Ms. Rapscott held it up for the girls to see. "Look what I won, girls!"

"Wow!" they said.

"No, no, no." She shook her finger at them.

"You're supposed to say, *It could be better*," Ms. Rapscott corrected. She set the bird feeder down on her desk. "Remember?"

Bea, Mildred, Annabelle, and Dahlia looked at one another, a little puzzled, and mumbled, "It could be better."

"Really, how?" Ms. Rapscott folded her arms and tilted her head.

Bea tried to think of what would have been better than a bird feeder. "It could've been a unicorn!"

"Or a pirate costume," Annabelle called out.

"Or a candy tree," Mildred shouted.

"Plus there's no birdseed with it," Dahlia pointed out.

Ms. Rapscott's shoulders sagged. "No birdseed? Now we have to go out in this . . . ow . . . storm . . . ow . . . and get some." She shrugged into her raincoat and tied on her bonnet. "Come along, ow . . . girls."

Soon they were all in their raincoats and bonnets on their way to town in the wettest rain to buy birdseed.

"Ow . . . ow . . . ow . . ." Ms. Rapscott said as she walked. When they were almost there she stopped and stood by the side of the road next to a large puddle. "STEP THREE! In order to have a really bad day, stand next to a large puddle by the side of the road and wait for a truck to come by."

"But you'll get splashed," Annabelle said.

"And you'll be soaking wet!" Mildred added.

"I know!" Ms. Rapscott said. "It's one of the very best ways to have a bad day." As if on cue a large truck drove by and splashed Ms. Rapscott. She was drenched.

They continued on to the birdseed store in this fashion with Ms. Rapscott dripping wet and saying, "Ow," every few strides. When they arrived a clerk with large round spectacles dressed in red suspenders and a polka-dotted bow tie said, "Pebble in your shoe and soaked—having a bad day, Ms. Rapscott?"

"Yes," Ms. Rapscott said sadly. "*And* I won a bird feeder."

"And no birdseed with it, I'll bet." The clerk shook his head. "It could've been better, Ms. Rapscott."

"It should've been a unicorn," Bea said.

"Or a candy tree," Mildred said.

"Or a pirate costume," Annabelle said.

The clerk agreed. "I do have birdseed for you." He took a bag of it and set it on the counter with a thump. "But it could be better, Ms. Rapscott."

"It could? How?" she asked.

"There could be more . . . and it could be cheaper," the clerk explained.

"Thank you *so* much," Ms. Raspcott said, pleased. "That'll make my bad day even worse!"

Clark paid. The girls followed the teacher out of the store. "Ow . . . ow . . . ow," she grimaced with every step.

"Whatever you do don't take that pebble out of your shoe!" the clerk called after her.

"Ow. . . . Thank you, I won't!" she called back.

And when they got home they set up the bird feeder.

Bea stood back and looked. "It could have been bigger."

"And a better color," Annabelle commented.

"It should have a larger hook to hang on the tree," Mildred complained.

"You definitely could've won a better bird feeder," Dahlia added.

"This has been *such* a bad day . . . ow!" Ms. Rapscott said as soon as they were back in the classroom. She stood with her hands clasped in front of her, and the girls knew she was about to say something important. They took out their pencils.

"How to Make a Bad Day Good!" the teacher announced.

"STEP ONE: Remove the pebble from your shoe." She took off her boot, turned it upside down, and the pebble fell out.

"How's your foot?" Mildred asked.

Ms. Rapscott rubbed it. "It could be better,

Mildred, but thank you for asking." The teacher limped upstairs to her bedroom and the girls scurried after her. When she reached her room that was like the inside of a ship's cabin, Ms. Rapscott flopped in the chair by the woodstove and frowned. "I'm cold and I'm wet. My foot is sore and I have an inferior bird feeder."

"Here's a towel, Ms. Rapscott," Bea offered.

"And your slippers." Dahlia placed them on the floor by the teacher.

"Here's a blanket." Mildred handed it to Ms. Rapscott.

"And a pillow." Annabelle took it off the bed and placed it behind the teacher's back.

Lewis was ready with her hot water bottle. The girls gathered around with worried looks on their faces, waiting to see if anything had changed for the better.

"Is it a good day yet?" Bea asked hopefully.

"Not yet," Ms. Raspcott answered. "STEP TWO: A bad day can become good by saying: *It could be worse!*"

"It could be worse!" Mildred shouted, eager to make the day better.

"It could? How?" Ms. Raspcott asked.

"You could still have a pebble in your shoe," Bea suggested.

"That's true, Bea," Ms. Rapscott replied.

"You could still be wet and cold from being splashed," Annabelle reminded her.

"You could have a bird feeder without bird-seed," Dahlia added.

Ms. Rapscott sat up. "You're right, it *could* be worse."

They peeked out the window and saw a flock of bright green birds on the bird feeder. When they looked them up in Ms. Raspcott's bird book, they discovered they were the rare emerald-crowned green finch that only came just before something really good was about to happen. Then, because it was still a few hours till dinner, they practiced toasting marshmallows with the new set of toasting forks Ms. Rapscott had bought the other day. They sat before her little woodstove with the marshmallows turning a gooey golden brown, and before long they realized they were having a good day.

Even Annabelle, who always expected the worst, had to say, "This hasn't been such a bad day after all."

Chapter 18
GETTING USED TO DISAPPOINTMENTS

That night another hurricane blew onto the island. Ms. Rapscott said it was Cyrus, Known for His Ferocity, but he was also an old hurricane who tired easily. He was a lot more bluster than anything and by morning he would have exhausted himself and sputtered away. For now, though, he was outside making a terrible fuss, rattling the Great Rapscott sign, flapping the flag, and whirling round and round the lighthouse. The girls didn't mind. They lay awake snug in their canopied beds long after lights were out to talk about Fay.

Bea was propped up on three pillows, hugging

her knees. "Even Ms. Rapscott says it's hard to stay at The Top."

"Are you sure you're not just hoping Fay will get kicked out?" Dahlia said from her side of the room. She suspected that Bea was unhappy about Fay being the first one to The Top.

"I just think it's unfair she got there first without having to do anything!" Bea said forcefully.

"It's totally unfair," Annabelle replied. She took off her glasses and laid them on the nightstand. "But I'm ready to go. I know everything there is to know about attending a dinner party, and I'm sure I won't do anything wrong."

"I'm ready, too." Bea sounded confident. "I hope we go tomorrow."

"Tomorrow?" Mildred could feel her stomach drop.

"Yes. It's time. We've learned enough!" Bea could already see herself wearing the gold Rapscott Medal for Reaching The Top. It was bad enough that Fay had gotten there first. What if she got a medal and Bea didn't?

Mildred sat up with alarm, and the quilt she'd

been clutching fell away from her shoulders, "Do you really think we'll go tomorrow?"

"I sure hope so; I'm tired of waiting!" Bea punched her pillow.

But Dahlia had other concerns and had been worried for weeks. "I hope the boys are all right and that Mr. Everbest has found his boot."

"All you care about are those stupid boys," Bea said angrily.

"That's not true!" Dahlia shot back, but it surprised her to hear that Bea even cared. "It's just that he keeps losing the boys and . . . and . . . all that microwave popcorn can't be doing them any good."

"Well, I'm certainly not worried about those revolting boys." Annabelle yawned. Neither was Bea. Then both girls pulled their bed curtains shut and rolled over to go to sleep.

Over in the green bed Mildred tossed and turned all night, fearing that they would set off for The Top in the morning. In the yellow bed Dahlia continued to worry about Mr. Everbest and the boys.

The next morning Hurricane Cyrus had grown weary and retired out to sea like Ms. Rapscott had said he would. The sun peeped through clouds and in the light of day Bea's and Annabelle's hopes for an excursion seemed highly unlikely. Mildred felt relieved.

It would be a normal day at Great Rapscott School. They'd learn How to Squeeze an Orange, Do a Jumping Jack, and Pick an Apple. Then they'd have lunch where they'd learn: How to Use a Screwdriver and Catch a Frog. After that maybe they'd go to town and buy something they liked. Then they'd come home, have a lesson in Going Far, have tea and pie (because even birthday cake could be too much of a good thing), and try not to be busy for a couple of hours before they went to bed. Yes, just another day at Great Rapscott.

Mildred's sense of security would not last long.

Ms. Rapscott looked through her binoculars intently and when she put them down she seemed more excited than usual. "There's news!" she exclaimed.

When Mildred looked, Lewis was busying himself with backpacks. Clark was checking his watch. That could only mean one thing: They would be going to The Top this day.

The girls sat up with interest.

"Is it Fay?" Bea asked.

Ms. Raspcott broke into a wide grin, showing off her two front teeth that overlapped. "Oscar has reached The Top!"

Everyone gasped.

"Oscar?" Bea said incredulously. "Sickly, puny Oscar?"

"None other than!" Ms. Rapscott exclaimed.

Dahlia jumped up. "But did you see Mr. Everbest and the other boys?"

"I have not seen hide nor hair of them," Ms. Rapscott announced gleefully. It was so mysterious and there was nothing she loved better than a good mystery. "They could be almost anywhere . . . except at The Top."

Dahlia took her seat, more upset than ever.

Bea sat with her chin on her chest and scowled.

Ms. Rapscott raised an eyebrow. "A Rapscott

Girl is always happy for another's achievements, Bea."

"I'm happy," Bea said unhappily, because having a boy get there before her was awful.

Ms. Rapscott's face lit up. She leaned over the short round girl to get a better look at her. "Are you . . . *disappointed*?"

"Yes." Bea sniffed. She could have even cried. "I'm so disappointed."

Of course there was hardly anything that Ms. Rapscott loved more than a good disappointment. She loved it more than heaps of snow, or hurricanes, or even a bad day, or a good mystery because if something was easy to do where was the FUN in that? Ms. Rapscott hopped once for joy. "Cheer up, Bea! There's nothing that will get you to The Top faster than a good disappointment."

Bea didn't think so. Annabelle was skeptical. Mildred was afraid. Dahlia was anxious to get to The Top and find Oscar to hear about what had happened to the others.

Ms. Rapscott explained, "Girls of Busy Parents are disappointed 97.2 percent of the time, class. Be aware that as a daughter of busy parents you will have MORE than your fair share of disappointments. And so . . . in order To Go Far in Life You Must Get Used to Disappointment."

Ms. Rapscott yanked on her raincoat and grabbed her backpack.

"But it's sunny today." Annabelle couldn't understand why they'd be needing raincoats.

Ms. Rapscott paid no attention to Annabelle and flung open the door to march outside. The girls wiggled into their raincoats and backpacks. They scrambled after the curious teacher just to see what she would do next.

The girls followed Ms. Raspcott and Lewis and Clark away from the lighthouse, all wondering what could be in store for them. The prospect of being disappointed was something none of them was looking forward to.

"Keep your eyes open, girls!" Ms. Raspcott called back to them.

"For what?" Mildred asked warily.

"For signs of The Top, what else?" she answered.

They hadn't gone far when Bea shouted, "Look!" Sure enough there was a sign stuck in the grass that said:

Straight to The Top

The road spiraled around and around up a mountain. Bea took the lead, while Ms. Rapscott, Lewis and Clark, and the rest of the girls followed behind.

The way was narrow with brightly colored cottages that had been built close to the road. Baskets of flowers hung from porches and box-wood bushes lined the cobbled walks. Bea looked for The Top, but it remained shrouded above in the mist. "Is it far?" she asked.

"It's very far," Ms. Rapscott answered.

When they turned a corner they passed a man coming from the opposite direction. He was tall, dark, and handsome and dressed in a long coat that went down to the ground, high boots that went up to his knees, and a top hat on his head. "Well, well! If it isn't Ms. Rapscott!" he bellowed.

"You're looking very dashing, indeed." The

headmistress seemed to know the man. "Say hello to the Adventurer, girls," she sang out.

"Getting used to disappointment, I see!" he said with a raucous laugh.

"Yes, we are," Ms. Rapscott replied. "We cannot get to The Top until then."

"You're certainly going in the right direction because you'll *never* get there—though you might get a hat." The handsome man straightened his on his head and flashed Ms. Rapscott a dazzling white grin.

The headmistress smiled back. "I'm sure you'll go very far in that hat."

He tipped it rakishly and clicked his heels. "And I'm sure you'll get used to disappointment." Then he turned and strode down the hill, whistling a merry tune.

Bea, Mildred, Annabelle, and Dahlia walked several more turns around the mountain that became ever steeper where the cottages had thinned out. There was another sign stuck in the ground that said:

Scenic Route

"Scenic route?" Bea said with disbelief. "But back there it said Straight to The Top!"

"But it *is* scenic," Ms. Rapscott said. In fact the view was spectacular. Lewis pointed out sights, and Clark took pictures. They were surrounded by mountains and could even see snowy Mt. Everbest. It looked close enough to touch. But The Top was still far, far away.

"I can't wait to see Oscar," Dahlia said to Mildred. She hoped he could tell her where the other boys were.

But Mildred had her own worries. For now she was keeping up, but every time she searched for The Top her heart sank. It was so far off it was barely visible. To make matters worse the road was becoming steeper with every turn, and she was already tired. Would she make it all the way up there? Or would they have to leave her like they almost did at The Bottom?

Suddenly a bicycle zoomed around the corner, and they all jumped to the side of the road. The rider was a young woman with curly red hair, wearing a wet suit with flippers on her feet and a top hat on her head. "Hello, Ms. Rapscott!"

The headmistress seemed to know this person as well. "And how are your dolphins doing?" Ms. Rapscott inquired.

"They said to say hello," the young woman replied cheerfully.

"Do say hello back, will you?" Ms. Rapscott replied.

"I will!" the young woman promised and then became serious. "But I hope you're not trying to get to The Top today, Ms. Rapscott."

"And why is that?" Ms. Rapscott asked.

"I'm so disappointed." The young woman sighed.

"We are too," Mildred said. "But we're trying to get used to it."

"I'm relieved to hear that," the woman said. "I'd hate to see you be disappointed when you didn't get there."

Ms. Rapscott agreed and the red-haired woman got back on her bike.

"I hope you go far," Ms. Rapscott said.

"I hope you get used to being disappointed!" The young woman in the wet suit waved and rode away on her bike.

The girls continued upward, glancing at one another anxiously. None of them knew what the red-haired woman could possibly mean. Where was The Top? How far-off could it be? It wasn't until they'd gone several more turns around the mountain that they came to a halt.

There it was.

The girls shaded their eyes and craned their necks to see the dazzling silhouette of a structure that stretched up into the sky and disappeared in the clouds. They stood motionless in awe of the sheer size and wonder of the many towers connected by sweeping arches. Tall windows glittered and winked in the sunlight.

"It's so beautiful," Bea whispered. Despite the steep grade she took off at a trot, eager to get there. The others followed. Even Mildred breathlessly hurried to meet up with Fay and finally see the candy tree and take a ride on the Ferris wheel!

Bea pumped her arms and pushed her little

legs as hard as she could. She was almost there! The girls came around the last corner only to be brought up short by a barrier that blocked the road. Standing before it was a short round guard in a gold uniform, wearing a tall, pointy gold hat, eating a cracker with a cube of cheese on it.

Bea narrowed her eyes. "You're the reception-ist from The Bottom."

The little woman chewed and swallowed her snack then brushed some crumbs off her chest. "I'm not *just* the receptionist from The Bottom," she said testily. "I'm the gatekeeper for The Top as well."

"She's right, class," Ms. Rapscott said, and the corgis indicated as much.

"Have you paid your dues?" the gatekeeper asked.

"Oh yes." Ms. Rapscott chuckled. "The *dues*."

The little woman closed her eyes and nodded. "No one gets to The Top without paying them."

Bea pushed herself around her classmates and stood face-to-face with the gatekeeper. "Fay didn't pay any dues!"

The gatekeeper flicked a stray crumb from the side of her mouth, "She didn't have to."

Bea stood her ground. "But you just said everyone has to."

"Everyone does," the gatekeeper replied. "Still there are some who never do pay their dues—and there is nothing you can *do* about it."

"But that's not fair!" Bea stamped a foot.

"It's also very disappointing." Ms. Rapscott looked sad and so did Lewis and Clark. The headmistress asked, "Will a bow do for dues?"

"A bow will do." The gatekeeper smiled.

Ms. Rapscott bowed deeply. "Bow to the gatekeeper, girls."

They grumbled and none of them wanted to but of course they did because Ms. Rapscott had told them to.

"Thank you," the gatekeeper said. "You have officially paid your dues—NOW GO AWAY!" she yelled. "THE TOP IS CLOSED!"

Ms. Rapscott made a little hop for joy. "This is even more of a disappointment than I thought it'd be."

The guard chased them away. "GO HOME! SHOO!"

Just then the sun went in. The clouds came out.

The girls backed up, almost too shocked to even run. How could they be turned away now? They'd even paid their dues! Bea sat down by the side of the road in the rain with her chin in her hands. She was more disappointed than she'd ever been in her entire life.

Chapter 19
ALMOST TO THE TOP

"Tickets? Get your tickets!" a voice shouted. The girls followed the voice that was coming from a small road that branched off, and just around the corner was a rickety-looking wooden stand and an elaborate sign that read:

Almost to The TOP
Go Far in Our TOP HATS!

Behind the stand was the same little woman in the gold uniform and tall pointy hat. "Tickets?"

Bea was tired of this woman who seemed to be everywhere. She marched up to her and said, "I thought you were the gatekeeper for The Top."

"I was, *and* the receptionist for The Bottom, and *now* I'm the ticket seller for Almost to The Top. I'm in charge of everything!" she exclaimed, and her chest swelled with pride.

"But how come?" Mildred asked.

"Because if I weren't you wouldn't have to be nice to me," the woman replied simply.

"But I don't want to be nice to you," Bea blurted out. In fact she felt like kicking her in the shins.

Sensing this, Ms. Rapscott stepped in. "We must be nice to people we meet on the way up if we want to go far, girls."

"Even if we don't feel like it?" Bea grumbled.

"Even if we don't feel like it," Ms. Rapscott replied.

Annabelle was fuming and had just about enough of this nonsense. First they go all the way to The Top to get used to being disappointed only to be disappointed that The Top is closed and now she had to be *nice*? It was outrageous. "Now, listen here." Annabelle narrowed her eyes in a not nice way at the ticket seller. "You just said The Top was closed."

"The Top *is* closed," the little woman answered. "Tickets are for *Almost* to The Top." She took off her hat with a sweeping gesture and offered Annabelle the inside of it. "Ticket?"

"How much?" Ms. Rapscott asked.

"One bow each!" the ticket seller said.

Ms. Rapscott bowed again and so did Lewis and Clark. "Bow to the ticket seller, class," Ms. Raspcott instructed.

"Again?" Bea said incredulously.

"Again!" Ms. Rapscott said cheerfully, and of course Bea and the other girls had no other alternative but to bow. "We'll take seven," the headmistress replied.

Satisfied with all the bows the little woman held out her hat where there were exactly seven tickets. "Follow the road to Almost to The Top."

"Thank you so much!" Ms. Rapscott bowed again. "You've been ever so nice."

When they'd gone a distance Bea walked up

beside the headmistress to complain. "She wasn't *that* nice."

"Yes, and why did *we* have to be nice?" Annabelle was still mad about that.

Ms. Rapscott smiled. "It's not easy for someone to be in charge of everything, Annabelle. The uniform is hot and I've heard itchy, too. And the hat is quite heavy—it makes the people wearing it rather cranky, and we should take that into consideration."

Then Ms. Rapscott and Lewis and Clark continued cheerfully up the hill taking in the stunning view. "A Rapscott Girl is always considerate, class!"

Bea was too disappointed to be considerate and walked glumly behind poky Mildred. All Bea could think about was that they would never get to The Top now. All their work this entire semester had been for nothing.

Mildred, Annabelle, and Dahlia were feeling just as badly. They wouldn't get to see Fay, or Oscar; there would be no candy tree, or ride on a Ferris wheel, or dinner parties, no unicorn named Twinkle Toes. There would be no gold medal with a diamond in the center.

Mildred moped listlessly up the road. "Ms. Rapscott always said that The Top was hard to get to."

"But we showed we had grit," Dahlia said vehemently. "And patience and kindness and we were all brave—all the right things that Ms. Rapscott said it took to get there!"

"We even paid our dues!" Annabelle cried.

"And bowed!" Bea added.

Dahlia shook her head. She hadn't wanted to bow, either, which is how it is when you have a lot of grit.

The girls made the final turn to Almost to The Top and were disappointed even more to see an old wooden shack with a sagging porch that looked just as rickety as the ticket stand. A small sign hung lopsided with blinking lights, only half of which still blinked, that said: Almost to The Top.

"This is it?" Bea groaned. It was the final insult to a long day of bitter disappointments.

Dahlia stood with her hands on her hips and said, "It's nothing but a dump."

"Never judge the inside of things by its outside," Ms. Rapscott remarked. Lewis wrote it down to use for a Remark of the Day in the future, and Clark noted the time that Ms. Rapscott had said it. "Come along, class," she called to them, and then disappeared inside through a screen door.

All four girls wanted nothing at this point but to go back to Great Rapscott School, have lunch, and learn a lesson like the Best Way to Make Fluffy Rice or How to Treat the Mumps.

They shuffled inside. Their eyes traveled around the small room from the ceiling to the floor; on shelves, tables, and hanging from hooks on the walls were hundreds of shiny black top hats.

But that was not the biggest surprise. Standing with her back to them at a full-length mirror was a girl with socks around her ankles trying on hats.

"Fay?" Bea said incredulously.

The girl turned around and her face broke into a huge grin. "Bea!" she shouted. "And Mildred and Annabelle and *Dahlia*! Finally Dahlia!"

The girls ran to her, overjoyed to see their classmate at last. They asked her a hundred questions, all talking at the same time. Bea stood back to get a good look at Fay to see if she was any different. She was dressed in her uniform and her two front teeth still stuck out, but her limp blond hair was limper than usual, and her eyes had even lost some of their sparkle. She looked unhappy.

"But, Fay, what are you doing here?" Bea exclaimed.

"We thought you were at The Top!" Mildred said.

Fay looked down. "I got kicked out."

"You put your forehead on the table, didn't you?" Annabelle said sternly. "Or you tried to eat your soup with your fork." She knew it'd be just like Fay to do something wrong like that.

"Worse," Fay said dully. "I talked about my knee socks, and they said I was boring."

"Tsk, tsk, tsk." Ms. Rapscott shook her head. "You must try to be more interesting, Fay."

Fay glanced at the teacher guiltily. "But that's not why I got kicked out—it was because of something else."

Just then a small figure stepped out of the shadows. He looked pale and unwell.

"Oscar!" Dahlia rushed to the boy. "I thought you were at The Top."

"I was." Oscar sniffed loudly and looked very unwell. "All of us boys were trying to get there. I-I couldn't keep up and got separated from them, and somehow I found my way to The Top all by myself."

Fay explained, "It was lonely there, and I was so happy to see Oscar. At first we had a lot of fun playing, but then he wanted to ride Twinkle Toes."

"She wouldn't let me, Ms. Rapscott," Oscar grumbled.

Ms. Rapscott shook her head sympathetically.

"All I did was tell him to get his own unicorn," Fay said defensively. "Then he started to cry!"

"She called me stupid," Oscar said sadly.

"And we had a fight." Fay pushed her bottom lip forward and blew a strand of hair that was in her eyes. "Then I got unhappy."

"So did I," Oscar added.

"We were told to leave," they said at the same time.

"Thanks to you," Fay said sharply.

Oscar's lower lip began to tremble and his eyes filled with tears.

Fay continued. "All you had to do was ask and they would've given you your own unicorn. You're so STUPID!"

Oscar gasped. "I'm not stupid!"

"You are—and if it weren't for you I'd still be at The Top!" Fay shouted.

Oscar's face suddenly went white. Fay looked on in shock as he slid to the floor and didn't move. "Is he dead?" she cried.

"Oscar!" Dahlia screamed. "What's wrong?"

Even Annabelle and Bea were worried because over the course of the semester, little by little, they too had begun to learn How to Feel Sorry for Someone Besides Themselves.

Bea and Annabelle glanced at each other tensely. They had a hunch that they knew what was wrong.

Bea leaned over the stricken boy. "Have you been feeling sorry for yourself lately?"

Oscar's eyes fluttered open. "Very."

Bea and Annabelle exchanged smiles, greatly relieved. Annabelle probed further. "And do you feel like you haven't a single friend in the whole world?"

"Yes—that's it exactly," Oscar replied.

Annabelle turned to Fay. "You see? He's not dead in the least!"

"He just has a case of Hurt Feelings," Bea said.

"A very bad case indeed!" Ms. Rapscott added.

Oscar closed his eyes again and lay still.

Fay looked on anxiously. "Is there a cure?"

"Yes," Ms. Raspcott said tentatively. "But I'm afraid it's something that you can only learn at The Bottom."

Fay had never been there, but it sounded awful. She bit her lip. She wrung her hands. "What shall we do?"

Ms. Rapscott and the corgis shook their heads. "We'll just have to leave him here . . ." she said sadly. "He'll most likely end up at The Bottom!"

"The Bottom!?" All five girls cried.

"Next to Making Mistakes and Trying Your Best at Being Your Worst, having Hurt Feelings is the best way to get there, you know," the teacher said.

Oscar began to sob uncontrollably. His shoulders shook, and it seemed like there was no comforting him.

"Oh, stop crying, Oscar." Annabelle knelt down by the boy's side. "Now listen to me. Fay didn't really mean it when she called you stupid."

"I didn't," Fay said.

"You didn't?" Oscar wiped his tear-stained face with his sleeve.

"No!" Fay shook her head vehemently.

"Are you sorry you said that, Fay?" Mildred had to know because she remembered how sorry she had felt for Dahlia when she first came to school and everyone was being mean to her.

Fay paused to think about it because she'd

never really felt sorry for anyone but herself, but Mildred was absolutely right! Fay knelt down by Oscar's side as well. "I'm *very* sorry—I really am, Oscar."

But there was still something wrong. He hadn't been entirely cured and Annabelle and Bea knew it.

"Look, Annabelle," Bea said. "He still has the classic slump to his shoulders."

Annabelle saw it, too. "And there's the telltale lackluster sheen to his eyes."

Bea gritted her teeth and pressed her lips together. Even though she hated to admit it, she knew Oscar wasn't stupid and the only way to cure the boy was to tell him so. "Of course you're not really stupid, Oscar—I mean, you found your own way to The Top, didn't you?"

"That's right!" Fay exclaimed.

Oscar brightened. "I-I guess I did."

"How do you feel now?" Fay asked anxiously.

The lackluster sheen to his eyes had all but disappeared. "I feel better!" Oscar said in a stronger voice.

The girls helped him to his feet and Dahlia looked on with a sense of astonishment. She wasn't surprised that Mildred had helped, but Bea and Annabelle? Maybe they weren't so bad after all. . . .

"Thanks for curing Oscar," Dahlia said shyly.

Bea and Annabelle glanced at each other self-consciously. Girls of busy parents aren't used to being thanked. The two girls looked down and mumbled an embarrassed, "You're welcome." But both were thinking the same thing: Maybe Dahlia Thistle wasn't so bad after all.

"Another miraculous recovery!" Ms. Rapscott made a little hop for joy, and the corgis grinned.

"But, Oscar," Dahlia asked. "Where are the other boys and Mr. Everbest?"

"Mr. Everbest got busy and never noticed I got left behind," Oscar said. "I don't know what happened to the other boys . . . but I'm sure something terrible." Oscar gave Ms. Rapscott's sleeve a tug. "Mr. Everbest said you knew of two assistants—will they never be not busy?"

"They will never be not busy," Ms. Rapscott said firmly.

Oscar had a desperate look on his face. "Are you sure?"

"Yes," the headmistress said quite surely. "It's disappointing news but we must get used to it. I will go at once to tell Mr. Everbest again myself because clearly he is still hoping otherwise." With that Ms. Rapscott ordered the class to pick out their hats. Lewis and Clark went to each girl and checked to make sure they were fitted properly.

Once Ms. Rapscott was satisfied that they each had a top hat that fit they were told to put them in their backpacks. Then they were allowed to leave, all grumbling at the same time that except for finding Fay and curing Oscar, so far it had been a very disappointing day.

Chapter 20

STANLEY AND LIVINGSTON

It seemed there was no end to the disappointments this day.

It continued to rain as Lewis and Clark found a road that led from Almost to The Top right up to Mt. Everbest Academy, but as they climbed higher it began to snow.

"Mittens are in your pockets, girls!" Ms. Rapscott called back to them. But even with the mittens they were soon shivering inside their raincoats and bonnets.

"Boys are such a nuisance," Annabelle muttered. If it weren't for these boys they'd be on their way home right now and only a little late for their tea.

Dahlia walked next to Oscar, eager for information about the other boys. "How has it been?" she asked, almost afraid for what he might say. "I mean, since I've been gone?"

"It's been awful." Oscar sniffed loudly. He may have been cured of Hurt Feelings but his nose was still running like a faucet. Dahlia offered him a tissue because she'd finally learned to always carry some.

He blew his nose. "Mr. Everbest has been so intent on getting to The Top and so busy with the New Boys that there's been nothing to eat but popcorn and jelly sandwiches." He wheezed. "Nathan's always falling down because there's been no one around to tell him to stop running in circles and Ernest won't stop making rude noises."

Bea joined them and asked, "What about Ricky and Nicky?" The last time she saw the twins they were rubbing their wrists from where she'd tied them. "Did they ever make it back to Mt. Everbest?"

"Yes," Oscar said. "But then they snuck out one night and jumped off the top of the school and were lost in the snowdrifts for three days before Mr. Everbest noticed they was gone."

"Poor things!" Dahlia cried. "And Reggie?" He was Known for Holding His Breath whenever he didn't get his way.

Oscar continued wiping his nose every few feet. "He's turned purple . . . sniff . . . several times . . . there was no one . . . sniff . . . to tell him to stop holding his breath."

"And Theodore?" Dahlia inquired.

Oscar shook his head. "He made a terrible face and it got stuck that way for a week."

They had reached the summit and were at the solid oak door of the boys' school when Oscar said, "I'm afraid, Ms. Rapscott, that something awful has happened to Mr. Everbest and the boys!"

"We must brace ourselves for the worst, class," Ms. Rapscott intoned, and knocked on the door.

They waited and exchanged worried looks.

Ms. Rapscott knocked again but there was

still no answer. Just when they all began to think that something awful had happened, the door opened.

"Ms. Rapscott!" Mr. Everbest was wearing a heavy flannel bathrobe that went down to his ankles and boiled wool slippers. "Oscar! I've been looking all over for you, my boy!" the head-master exclaimed. He ushered them into the room that was round with seven desks in the center. On the walls were shelves that went all the way up to the ceiling filled with hundreds of books. There was a map of the mountain and a clock on the wall much like the one at Great Rapscott School.

Ms. Rapscott stood with her hands folded the way she always did whenever she had some-thing important to say, and she was just about to deliver her disappointing news when Mr. Everbest said, "I'm afraid I have the most dis-appointing news, Ms. Rapscott. While I was teaching them How to Go Far in Life I seem to have lost the boys!"

The girls gasped.

"Oh, that *is* disappointing," Ms. Rapscott replied. "What happened?"

"It was my ninety-ninth try for The Top, as you know, and I'd made up my mind that I was going to get there this time if it was last thing I did. With only one boot I went farther and farther, my sights set solely on The Top. Ricky and Nicky kept wandering off—but I was far too busy to teach them How to Find Your Way—and I lost track of them. Soon after, the other boys wandered off and I lost them as well. The Top was closed but that didn't stop me—I'd paid my dues and would not be turned away. The higher I went the worse the weather became, first with fog then with more snow than I'd ever seen. Still, I pressed on. Then I ran out of hot chocolate, and then crackers, and then cheese." Mr. Everbest sighed deeply. "And wouldn't you know, when the sky cleared and I looked, The Top was behind me—I'd gone right by it without even knowing. I said to myself, 'Everbest, you've gone too far!' Suddenly I was more tired than I'd ever been in my entire life, so I just sat down and must have fallen asleep right there in the snow."

"Did you by chance wake up in a bed like a boat?" Ms. Rapscott inquired.

"Not a boat but a sleigh!" Mr. Everbest said surprised. "How did you know?"

"Because the very same thing happened to me!" Ms. Rapscott said.

"I *failed* in the best possible way."

"Yes!" Mr. Everbest said. "It often happens when you Try to Go Far, doesn't it."

"Yes, it often does," Ms. Rapscott agreed. "But see here, Mr. Everbest, have you looked for the boys in their dormitory?"

"I have not—I was too afraid they would not be there." He definitely looked fearful.

"That would be an awful disappointment—but my girls here are learning how to get used to it," Ms. Rapscott said.

"Ah! Yes!" Mr. Everbest replied. "The fastest way to The Top—shall we go?" He was still afraid and led the way cautiously to the boys' dorm which was high atop a tower on the other side of the school. And when they'd reached the room he stopped and covered his eyes.

Ms. Rapscott peeked around the corner and her face lit up at what she saw. "You must come and look, Mr. Everbest!"

When he did the headmaster exclaimed, "Astounding!" because a fire burned brightly in the hearth and all the boys were snug in their bunk beds, right where they belonged.

Dahlia ran to her former classmates, shouting each of their names. The boys hopped out of their beds and surrounded her, all smiles and laughter.

"Did you ever find Harold?" Reggie asked anxiously.

Dahlia grinned and pulled the stuffed lamb out of her pocket.

"How did you get him back?" Oscar asked.

"Are you all right?" Theodore wanted to know. But before she could answer, the boys began to talk about all they'd done and where they'd been. They jabbered at once, each trying to sound braver than the next.

The girls hung back and watched Dahlia let the boys rattle on. She asked them questions and sounded interested, even though she hadn't had a chance to say much about herself. It was clear to see why the boys liked her so much—Dahlia was a good listener.

Bea was just about to point out to Annabelle that all the boys wanted to do was talk about themselves when Reggie exclaimed, "Dahlia, you've grown!" The other boys agreed because they could see that she reached almost up to Reggie's waist now.

Dahlia blushed and boasted, "I'm Head Girl, too!" She began telling the boys about her time at the girls' school. Bea braced herself, ready to hear Dahlia tell them how she'd been utterly ignored and left out.

But Dahlia never said a word about it. The boys roared with laughter as she told them how she'd been swept away on the end of a bunch of birthday balloons.

Bea turned to Annabelle. "Do you think she likes them better than us?"

"Probably," Annabelle said glumly. She wouldn't have blamed Dahlia, either, because she knew that she and Bea had been not nice to the new girl all semester.

Mr. Everbest and Ms. Rapscott remained in the doorway to the boys' dorm. The headmaster tilted his head in puzzlement. "May I ask, Ms. Rapscott, what brings you to Mt. Everbest on such a dark snowy night?"

"I'm afraid that I, too, have the most disappointing news, Mr. Everbest," Ms. Rapscott said sadly. "The two assistants that I mentioned in my letter will never be *not* busy!"

Mr. Everbest's face fell. "Well that is *frightfully* disappointing, but the fact is, I no longer need assistants."

At that very moment two small corgis waddled into the room.

"I had failed to realize that I'd gone too far, Ms. Rapscott, but luckily these two found me and brought me home in their sleigh that they turned into a bed!" Mr. Everbest explained.

"Why, it's Stanley and Livingston!" Ms. Rapscott made a little hop for joy. Lewis and Clark ran to them and shook their paws heartily.

"You've met?" Mr. Everbest asked surprised.

"Of course! They're Lewis and Clark's little brothers," Ms. Rapscott said.

"Right you are!" Mr. Everbest exclaimed. "Now I see the resemblance!"

Stanley came back into the room carrying a tray of hot chocolate, and Livingston had a platter of egg salad sandwiches with the crusts cut off. Lewis and Clark watched proudly as their little brothers went from boy to boy, then all the girls and Ms. Rapscott, expertly serving them. After that the four corgis gobbled up the rest of the sandwiches and warmed their paws by the fire.

Mr. Everbest offered Ms. Rapscott a seat, and when they'd finished eating he sat back and gave her a quizzical look. "Have you noticed, Ms. Rapscott, that we seem to have quite a bit in common?"

"I *have*, Mr. Everbest," Ms. Rapscott responded. "So coincidental that I have in my closet the very same fisherman's sweater, sturdy boots, and brown pants."

"It's extraordinary, really," the headmaster continued. "Let's see . . ." He began to count off on his fingers the number of similarities. "We both teach children of busy parents, we both like birthday cake and ice cream and hot chocolate . . . and egg salad sandwiches, too. And now we even both have corgis who wear fisherman's sweaters as our assistants."

Ms. Rapscott leaned forward and asked in a low voice, "But how about foul weather?" Very few people liked foul weather the way she did. Ms. Rapscott wouldn't have held it against the headmaster if he didn't.

"I *adore* foul weather, Ms. Rapscott!" Mr. Everbest made a sweeping gesture with his arm. "Why do you think I live on top of a snowy, dark, gloomy mountain such as this?"

Ms. Rapscott winked. "I half suspected, Mr. Everbest."

The headmaster studied the headmistress with what could only be described as amazement. "Do you think, Ms. Rapscott, that we should be . . . *friends*?"

"In actual fact, Mr. Everbest, I don't see how we could *not* be!" Ms. Rapscott said. The headmaster and the headmistress clinked their mugs.

The girls of course were all watching the exchange from their side of the room, and when Ms. Rapscott noticed they quickly looked away as if none of them had been eavesdropping. Lewis checked the time and Clark recorded it so that Ms. Rapscott and Mr. Everbest would always be able to look back on this moment and know the exact time and date that they became friends.

Meanwhile, the boys and girls were getting along beautifully. While they talked and drank their hot chocolate Ricky and Nicky asked Dahlia if her classmates were being any nicer to her.

"Yes," Dahlia said, and this time she didn't have to fib.

"It's better for us, too," Ricky glanced at his brother. "In fact we've decided that we're never going back."

"Home?" Dahlia asked surprised.

"We like it better here," the twins answered.

The other boys agreed.

Nathan said, "Our parents will never miss us."

Theodore added, "Mr. Everbest always says it's not that our parents don't love us—it's just that they're busy. But I'm not so sure."

"Ms. Rapscott says the same thing!" Annabelle rolled her eyes.

Theodore rolled his eyes, too. "I never want to go back home, either," he confided to Annabelle. "Do you?"

Annabelle shook her head. Theodore shook his head, too.

Annabelle smiled shyly and Theodore smiled shyly back.

The two were getting on surprisingly well.

Unfortunately, groups of boys and girls of busy parents have difficulty getting along with each other for any length of time. It wasn't long before Theodore, Oscar, Nathan, Ernest, Reggie, and Ricky and Nicky started to brag to Bea, Mildred, Fay, Annabelle, and Dahlia about how they'd gone far.

"We went farther than you!" Bea bragged back.

Ernest made a rude noise.

"Immature boys," Annabelle snapped. "Did you ever make it to The Top?"

Nathan, who had the lazy eye and long lifeline, frowned. "It was closed."

Theodore said, "We got to Almost to The Top."

"Did you get a hat?" Mildred asked.

"Of course we got a hat," Theodore and Ernest both said at once.

"Prove it!" Bea challenged the boys.

They became quiet. Ernest shrugged. "We don't have them anymore."

"Ha!" Bea exclaimed. "I knew you couldn't prove it."

By now Reggie's face was turning purple with anger, and he wasn't even holding his breath. "Dahlia! Why don't you ditch these dopey girls and come back to school with us!"

Then Ricky called Mildred, "Mildew," and Nicky called Bea, "Pee," and soon all the boys were jeering and calling, "Dopey Girls! Dopey Girls!"

Dahlia squinched up her face. She stamped

her foot and in her best Head Girl voice yelled, "They're not dopey girls!" She turned to her classmates, Bea, Mildred, Fay, and Annabelle. "They're Rapscott Girls—and if it weren't for them Oscar would be well on his way to The Bottom!"

Oscar swallowed hard. "She's right," he said sheepishly.

The boys were startled into silence.

Reggie pushed out his lower lip. "Then you're never coming back to school at Mt. Everbest, ever?"

Dahlia hesitated. She thought about all that had happened since she'd been shipped to Great Rapscott School. How she'd almost been left at The Bottom, but then how Annabelle had cured her of Hurt Feelings and Ms. Rapscott had made her Head Girl . . . how she had flown on the birthday balloons and how Mildred and the others had given up going to The Top because of her . . . and how Bea and Annabelle had cured Oscar as well. For the first time Dahlia thought that she actually felt more like a Rapscott Girl than an Everbest Boy.

The boys held their breath as they waited.

Dahlia finally said, "I'll never come back to school at Mt. Everbest."

Now even Bea had to admit that she could no longer hold it against Dahlia Thistle for being made Head Girl because she really did have grit—and lots of it. Of course Mildred had grown to like Dahlia early on and Fay still had to get to know her, but Annabelle found herself surprisingly relieved. By now she couldn't imagine Great Rapscott School without Dahlia Thistle.

"Promise you'll come for visits?" Reggie asked.

"Not just one," Oscar added.

"Lots and lots of visits," Nathan and Ernest called out.

"You have to promise." Ricky and Nicky sniffed because they were both almost ready to cry.

"And you'll bring Annabelle?" Theodore asked bashfully, and Annabelle's face turned red.

"I'll bring everybody!" Dahlia exclaimed. "I promise!"

To celebrate Stanley produced a bag of marshmallows, and Livingston had a set of toasting forks to go with them, but Ms. Rapscott rose from her seat to announce, "It's time to go, class!"

"Oh, *do* stay, Ms. Rapscott," Mr. Everbest said with great sincerity.

"Can't we toast just one marshmallow?" Mildred pleaded.

"Absolutely not." Ms. Rapscott gathered her things.

The girls all ran and pressed their noses to the window to see that it was snowing even harder than before, and they protested pitifully.

"A true Rapscott Girl never outwears her welcome." No matter how Mr. Everbest tried to assure her she was nowhere near outwearing her welcome the headmistress would not change her mind. "Raincoats on! Bonnets, too!" she said, and the girls knew there was no use in arguing.

Finally Ms. Rapscott leaned over Stanley and Livingston, for they were even shorter than Lewis and Clark. She looked into both their eyes. "I thought you would never be not busy," she said in a low voice, and the girls strained their ears to hear. The little corgis met Ms. Rapscott's gaze and twitched their noses. "But are you sure?" she asked, and they nodded. "You're quite sure that you've gone far enough and that you want to stay and that you will both be contented?" They nodded their heads positively that they were quite sure. "Right then!" Ms. Rapscott seemed satisfied with Stanley's and Livingston's answer.

She straightened up and tied on her rain bonnet. "You are in good hands, Mr. Everbest, and you should never be busy again," she said confidently, and stepped out into the night.

"I'm sure I won't be, Ms. Rapscott," Mr. Everbest called to her. "Come back soon!"

Chapter 21
Coming Home

Outside the boys' school the air was so cold that it took the girls' breath away. Clark checked his watch. It was 8:17—long past tea and almost the girls' bedtime. The snow was falling and the wind pulled furiously at their bonnets.

Mildred took one look at the deep drifts that blocked the way down and moaned. She knew that she would never be able to manage the difficult long walk back to school.

"I'm freezing!" Bea yelled over the wind. It blew around them and through their raincoats, chilling them to the bone. It seemed especially awful of Ms. Rapscott to make them walk home in such weather, and none of them liked her very much right now.

"I-I w-w-wish we were already b-back at our school," Dahlia said with chattering teeth.

Ms. Rapscott seemed completely unconcerned. "Top hats out, class!" she ordered, and placed hers squarely on her head. Lewis and Clark already had theirs on.

"Top hats?" It was hard to know if Annabelle's face was red from anger or the cold. "This is ridiculous! We need warm woolly hats!"

"It's not the least bit ridiculous, Annabelle," Ms. Rapscott said smoothly. "Clark? How long would it be before the girls all turn into blocks of ice even if they had on warm woolly hats? Fifteen minutes?" Clark nodded. "Ah! Just as I thought. Only a top hat will do right now." Ms. Rapscott straightened hers on her head and continued, "Inside your hats you will find the E-Z KWIK INSTRUCTIONS."

The girls looked and sure enough there was a small label stuck to the inside of their hats that read:

GO FAR IN A TOP HAT!

Directions:

STEP ONE: Take hat and stand in WIDE OPEN AREA

STEP TWO: Place hat on head

STEP THREE: Clearly state destination

"Top hats on, please!" Ms. Rapscott commanded. The girls put their top hats on their heads—even Annabelle, though she did roll her eyes.

"Hold hands, class!" the headmistress barked.

The girls stood shoulder to shoulder. Bea took Mildred's hand, Mildred took Fay's, Fay took Annabelle's, and Annabelle didn't think twice about taking Dahlia's hand—even if it turned out to be damp and squishy. Dahlia had chosen Great Rapscott over Mt. Everbest and now she was officially one of them. Bea reached out and took hold of Dahlia's hand as well, forming a circle. Dahlia held Bea's hand and smiled because she knew she was no longer the new girl. She was a Rapscott Girl.

"One . . . two . . . three . . ." Ms. Rapscott counted, and then asked, "Where do we want to go, class?"

"Home!" Bea shouted.

"And where is that—all together girls as loud as you can!" Ms. Rapscott sang out.

The girls took deep breaths and yelled, "Great Rapscott School for Girls of Busy Parents!"

It happened in the blink of an eye. One moment they were cold and miserable in the middle of a raging snowstorm, and the next they were in their own beds at school, cozy and warm, wearing their favorite pajamas!

They looked at one another in bewilderment and full of questions, but Ms. Rapscott was nowhere to be seen. Neither were their top hats. Bea jumped out of her bed to see if it had fallen underneath, then she threw back the covers to see if it was there. It was not.

"Mine's gone, too!" Mildred said, and so were all the others. The five girls started to talk at the same time. How had they gotten back to school?

"It was the hats—they were magic," Fay said excitedly.

"It's just another extremely strange phenomenon," Annabelle said astutely, "like the boxes."

The other girls nodded. They'd discussed it often because they'd all had the same suspicion whenever they traveled to and from school in them. There had been the telltale sound of the wind whistling outside, the definite sensation of swooping, turning, tumbling, as if they were inside a box that was . . . flying.

"The hats are definitely like the boxes," Annabelle concluded. Then she pushed her glasses up her nose. "And did you see Ms. Rapscott and Mr. Everbest talking at such great length to each other?"

"They decided to be *friends*." Bea wiggled her eyebrows.

"So what if they're friends?" Mildred said.

Annabelle rolled her eyes at Mildred for being so dense. "It's quite clear," she said knowingly, "that Ms. Rapscott and Mr. Everbest are meant for each other."

Mildred's eyes grew large, "You don't mean . . . ?"

Annabelle sniffed. "It's terribly romantic— just like Romeo and Juliet!"

Bea wrinkled her nose. "Who are they?"

"They're star-crossed lovers," Annabelle said dreamily. "I read all about them in the *Encyclopedia Britannica*." She held a hand over her heart and recited, "'Oh Romeo, Romeo . . . wherefore art thou Romeo'?"

"Oh Theodore, Theodore . . . wherefore art thou Theodore!" Bea imitated Annabelle. Dahlia and Mildred held a hand over their mouths and giggled.

"Don't be ridiculous!" Annabelle tossed her head, though she did think that of all those revolting boys he was the least revolting. She continued. "And did you see Ms. Rapscott speaking with Mr. Everbest's corgis before we left?"

The other girls had seen and thought it odd as well. Annabelle eagerly added, "I distinctly heard Ms. Rapscott ask them, 'Are you quite sure you've gone far enough?'"

"Very good, Annabelle," Ms. Rapscott said. "I see you were paying attention." She came down the spiral stairs and entered the room. Under her arm was a large book. She sat on Bea's bed with it on her lap, and the other girls gathered around to see. It was bound in leather that was old and cracked. Engraved in gold were the names:

LEWIS AND CLARK

"You may not know it," Ms. Rapscott began, "but Lewis and Clark had parents who were busy, too. They were very famous show dogs who won nearly every blue ribbon and trophy that two corgis could. But of course they were too busy to look after Lewis and Clark and their little brothers, Stanley and Livingston." Ms. Rapscott blew dust off the book and opened it to a page with a faded picture of four dogs wearing backpacks studying a map.

"When they were little, Lewis and Clark were forever wandering off, getting caught in storm drains and plummeting out of the back of pickup trucks. They lived by their wits from a very young age and finally, when they were old enough, they took their little brothers and wandered off for good."

Ms. Rapscott turned the pages and the girls climbed onto the bed and crowded closer to get a better look.

One photo showed four corgis standing on a raft, guiding it with long poles down a wide muddy river. On another page they were hiking up the side of a volcano with streams of red-hot steaming lava behind them. There was a photo of them sticking a flag on the top of a mountain, leading camels through a desert, and sailing a boat across an angry slate gray ocean. Ms. Rapscott turned page after page of yellowed and torn newspaper clippings that heralded, **"CORGIS ROUND CAPE!" "CORGIS CROSS THE CONGO!" "CORGIS CLIMB KILIMANJARO!"**

"Wow," Fay whispered.

"Lewis and Clark were famous explorers!" Even Annabelle was impressed. She had read of many explorers in her *Encyclopedia Britannica*, but none of them were corgis.

The girls had always known that Lewis and Clark were special but never imagined they'd traveled so far, though it seemed feasible given how quickly they could put things in a backpack and make hot chocolate.

Ms. Rapscott continued. "It was on one of their journeys that they found me! I had gone too far, girls. It's possible to do, you know. I had *failed* to realize it before it was too late. The corgis brought me home in their boat and turned it into a bed. They fed me soup until I recovered and was back to my old self. Then we fell into a happy routine, and Lewis and Clark gave up their travels to live with me. They had gone quite far enough, girls, because they had found what they were looking for."

"What were they looking for, Ms. Rapscott?" Mildred asked.

"A home," Ms. Rapscott replied.

"But what about Stanley and Livingston?" Bea asked.

"They still wanted to Go Far in Life," Ms. Rapscott replied. "One night they wandered off and never came back. We received many Friendly Letters from the far corners of the world—they went even farther then Lewis and Clark could have ever dreamed. We invited them many times for a visit to Great Rapscott but they were always busy. Finally they agreed to come and were on their way here when they found Mr. Everbest."

"But, Ms. Rapscott." Annabelle was still puzzled. "It looked like they were telling you something tonight—what did they say?"

"That they had gone quite far enough." Ms. Rapscott closed the photo album with a snap and a puff of dust. "And that they now know the best part of Going Far is coming home."

The girls knew this, too—especially Fay—and when she yawned Ms. Rapscott stood. "I'm quite sure that you must all be very sleepy after such a busy day." With that she marched up the spiral stairs and was gone.

Suddenly they all *were* very sleepy. They snuggled under the covers happy to be in their own beds back at the school that felt more like home than their real homes. As they drifted off to sleep not one of the girls felt the least bit of disappointment, even after an entire day of it.

Chapter 22
GREAT RAPSCOTT DAY

The girls were very happy to have Fay back with them again. One of the first things they did was to fill her in on the mysterious seventh floor.

"I didn't even know there was a seventh floor!" she said, surprised.

"Neither did we," Bea said. "But it's off-limits."

"And we don't know what's up there," Mildred added. "Annabelle thinks it could be a giant spider in a cage."

Annabelle rolled her eyes. "I was just kidding, Mildred!"

Mildred laughed uneasily at her own silliness to believe such a thing, but she was not alone in thinking that anything in the world could be up there on the seventh floor.

It was already November. Hurricane Daisy had come to stay at Great Rapscott, but she was a pleasant storm with rain that tasted like lemonade and the girls didn't mind her too much. The entire week Ms. Rapscott kept them on their toes with lessons, especially Fay who was behind in her studies and had to work hard to catch up. They learned how to use a salad spinner, dig a hole, and skip a stone. They were taught how to do a somersault, build a fort out of blankets, and play tag. They wrote essays and had round table discussions on everything from how to crochet a pot holder to the best way to treat poison ivy.

They went into town to buy something that they liked as often as possible and had lunch at the Big White Lighthouse Luncheonette, making sure not to order the same thing twice.

By now the girls were anxious to know: Had they passed or failed the course HOW TO GO FAR IN LIFE? Even though they hadn't actually reached The Top, except for Fay, would they each receive the gold medal anyway? Ms. Rapscott was not ready to tell them and the girls knew that it was useless to keep asking.

It wasn't until the end of the week as Hurricane Daisy was on her way out that the headmistress had an announcement to make. At Morning Meeting Clark stood by the chalkboard with his pointer, and Ms. Rapscott stood silently with her hands folded in front of her until there was total quiet in the classroom. The girls sat tensely in their seats.

"Tradition!" The headmistress paused and looked them right in the eye for emphasis. "Here at Great Rapscott School we have a tradition every November tenth called Great Rapscott Day." She wrote in big letters on the chalkboard and then underlined it with a flourish.

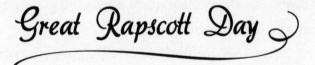

Great Rapscott Day

Clark pointed to it. The headmistress spoke, "It is on Great Rapscott Day that we have the Great Medal Ceremony where you will learn if you have passed or failed the course HOW TO GO FAR IN LIFE."

The girls started talking excitedly because this was just what they'd been waiting to hear.

"It is on Great Rapscott Day," Ms. Rapscott spoke over them in a stern voice, and they became quiet, "that we have the Great Open House!"

Bea scrunched up her nose. "What's that?"

"It is a day for your parents to come to Great Rapscott School and meet the students and faculty on campus." Ms. Rapscott paused and breathed deeply through her large nose. "The value of the Great Open House cannot be over-emphasized."

Dahlia Thistle immediately raised her thin arm and waved her tiny hand. "But Ms. Rapscott . . . I think my parents are too busy to come to the Great Open House."

"Precisely, Dahlia!" Ms. Rapscott exclaimed. "*All* of your parents are too busy to come—which is why we will send them a written *un*invitation NOT to." She snapped her fingers. "Clark, take a note, please."

Ms. Rapscott paced as she dictated.

Dear Parents,

We understand that you are too busy to come to our Great Open House so you are cordially NOT invited to come on November 10th at 11:00 a.m.

Coffee and birthday cake will be served while you are not here.

Sincerely,

Ms. Rapscott

HEADMISTRESS
GREAT RAPSCOTT SCHOOL FOR GIRLS OF BUSY PARENTS
BIG WHITE LIGHTHOUSE BY THE SEA

Clark trotted away to make copies and mail the *un*invitations. Ms. Rapscott had one more festivity to explain. "On Great Rapscott Day we also have a sacred tradition where students are allowed up to the seventh floor."

The girls gasped and began to chatter excitedly about what could be up there, but Ms. Rapscott asked for quiet. "Shh . . . Shh . . . no more talking!"

There was much to do to get ready for Great Rapscott Day. The classroom needed to be tidied up, the silverware and the old-fashioned silver coffeepot needed to be polished, the good china cups and plates needed to be taken out, and the white tablecloth and napkins needed to be ironed. It wasn't until the girls were in their beds that night that they had time to themselves, and they stayed up late to talk.

Fay was Known for Having an Adventurous Spirit and was intrigued by the notion of a mysterious floor that they were never allowed to go to. "I'll bet it's a scary old attic with a ghost!"

"Or green goblins!" Bea added.

"Or ghosts, green goblins, and skeletons!" Fay said breathlessly.

"That would be so cool." Bea had missed Fay's spunk.

"Stop it, you guys, that's scary," Mildred cried.

"That's silly." Annabelle huffed. "There's no such thing as ghosts, green goblins, or skeletons, and even if there were why would we need to see them in some stupid old attic on Great Rapscott Day?" Annabelle arranged her blankets. "No. It's something far more special." Annabelle sniffed. "Like a fabulous library."

"Or maybe a room with a candy tree?" Mildred hoped.

Annabelle rolled her eyes. "Or maybe a flying car."

"Yeah, a flying car!" Fay called out.

"I was *kidding*, Fay," Annabelle said drily.

Fay ignored Annabelle. "Or maybe there's a swimming pool on the seventh floor—like the one they had at The Top with a waterfall and a slide!"

Dahlia covered Harold because she felt a draft and suddenly thought of something. "Maybe Ms. Rapscott's brothers or sisters live up there."

"Or maybe it's a magic potion room," Bea called out.

"There are no brothers or sisters and there's no such thing as a magic potion room! It's a library!" Annabelle was annoyed because the girls were being ridiculous. "Listen to me!" She had something far more important for them to discuss. "Never mind the seventh floor! Do any of you realize that none of us—except for Fay—has passed the course this semester?"

The room became very quiet as each girl considered the possibility.

Bea couldn't stand the thought. "Do you really think we . . . *failed*?"

"We never did get to The Top," Annabelle said bluntly.

"I did!" Fay called from her side of the room.

"But you didn't stay there," Bea reminded her.

"Yes, I did," Fay said sharply. "Until I got unhappy."

Dahlia nodded. "You should get a medal for sure."

"Yes," Annabelle said. "Technically, Fay should get a medal—and besides, it wasn't so easy being there all that time. It was lonely and she was always worrying about staying happy."

"That's right!" Fay called out.

Bea rested her chin on her chest and scowled. "I don't think she should."

"Why not?" Fay didn't like that Bea hadn't given her any credit at all for at least staying at The Top a little while.

"Because you never went to The Bottom—you got to go straight to The Top and you only got there by mistake," Bea pointed out. "And you didn't even pay any dues."

"So what?" Fay said, her voice rising.

"It's not fair," Bea complained.

"It's totally fair!" Fay cried.

"Stop arguing!" Dahlia called from her bed.

"I'm going to sleep!" Annabelle shouted, and pulled her curtains shut.

"Good night!" Bea yelled, and pulled her curtains shut.

Mildred and Dahlia said good night softly to each other, still wondering if they had passed or failed.

Great Rapscott Day dawned cool and calm and all the girls woke up with butterflies in their stomachs. They hurried to get dressed, avoiding the touchy subject of the previous night, and skipped down the stairs to Morning Meeting.

Lewis and Clark had already set the large old-fashioned-looking silver coffeepot on Ms. Rapscott's desk that had been covered with the white tablecloth. The china cups and plates and the silver forks and spoons, as well as cloth napkins, were all arranged neatly. Ms. Rapscott carried a cake platter with a beautiful extra-large twelve-tiered birthday cake that was iced with pink frosting. "Happy Great Rapscott Day, class!" she sang out, and then set the cake on the desk, brushed off her hands, and straightened a row of forks.

The girls stood in a group not knowing what to do, this being their first ever Great Rapscott Day.

Mildred whispered to Fay, "I really hope Ms. Rapscott doesn't think our parents are coming after all."

"I hope not, too," Fay replied. "Before I left mine couldn't even remember my name."

"Mine thought I was going to camp," Mildred said.

"Mine didn't even know that I almost got thrown in a garbage truck," Bea chimed in.

"You did?" Fay asked, forgetting that she was still mad at Bea for not giving her any credit for getting to The Top and staying there.

Bea nodded. "I'll tell you all about it later." She hoped that maybe they had sort of made up, but more than that she was relieved that Fay hadn't come down with a case of Hurt Feelings over the incident.

Just then there was a knock at the door and all five girls held their breath. Lewis and Clark opened the door and there stood a rotund man with a mustache and a very important-looking sash across his chest.

"What ho, Ms. Rapscott!" he bellowed, and entered the room. "Happy Great Rapscott Day!"

"Look, girls, it's our mayor. Say hello!" Ms. Rapscott bustled over to the large man and pumped his hand.

"Hello, Mayor," the girls said shyly.

"Louder!" Ms. Rapscott cupped an ear. "A

Rapscott Girl is always exuberant on Great Rapscott Day!"

"Hello, Mayor!" the girls called out exuberantly.

He hastily said hello on his way to the refreshment table where Lewis poured his coffee and Clark stood ready with a large slice of cake. "Did they make it to The Top?" he asked loudly.

"No, but the girls did make it to Almost to The Top," Ms. Rapscott replied.

The mayor ate the frosting first then he started on the cake. A piece of it teetered on his fork as he asked, "Did they get a hat?"

"Oh yes," Ms. Rapscott said with a look of pride at her girls.

The mayor seemed pleased and popped the cake in his mouth. "Then it was all worth it!" He dabbed his lips. "I do love Great Rapscott Day!"

"More cake?" Ms. Rapscott inquired.

"Yes, please," the mayor answered. "And you know, Ms. Rapscott, just the teeniest, tiniest bit of ice cream would be marvelous with this cake!"

While Lewis and Clark ran to get some, there was another knock at the door.

A little round woman in a sparkly gold uniform and a pointy gold hat as tall as she was strolled into the classroom and nodded, "Happy Great Rapscott Day, Ms. Rapscott."

"Say hello, girls," the headmistress prompted her class, but the girls weren't sure what to call this woman.

Bea wrinkled her nose. "Are you the receptionist?"

Mildred tilted her head. "Or the gatekeeper?"

Annabelle and Fay were equally perplexed. "Or the ticket seller?"

"Or what?" Dahlia shrugged.

The little woman pushed back her shoulders and her chest puffed up with pride. "I am the Lady in Gold."

"HELLO, LADY IN GOLD!" the girls called out exuberantly, remembering that they were supposed to be exuberant today.

"Hello." The little woman sniffed and sashayed over to the refreshments table.

"Do we have to bow, too?" Bea asked, hoping she didn't.

"Not today." The Lady in Gold dismissed the

question with a wave of her hand. "I'm terribly fatigued." She collapsed in a chair and tried to take off her hat but it wouldn't budge. "Would you mind, Lewis? It's so heavy," she said dolefully. The corgi struggled to lift the hat off her head, and it was only with Clark's help that the two succeeded. They set it down with a loud *THUD!*

Ms. Rapscott shook her head, "It's not easy being in charge of everything, is it?"

"No, Ms. Rapscott." The Lady in Gold sighed. A corgi handed her a dish of ice cream and birthday cake.

"But I do hope you don't get too busy!" The headmistress waggled a finger at the little woman.

"Busy? Never!" she said indignantly. "I was taught better than that, Ms. Rapscott, wasn't I?" She winked and gobbled up her birthday cake with gusto.

Just then a jogger, a woman pulling a wagon full of pumpkins, and a policeman entered the room. "Happy Great Rapscott Day! Happy Great Rapscott Day!" the parrot on the woman's shoulder squawked.

"Happy Great Rapscott Day to you, too." Ms. Rapscott shook the parrot's wing and walked the little group over to the refreshment table.

The woman watched with delight as Clark cut her an extra-large piece of cake—enough for both her and her parrot. She winked at Ms. Rapscott.

"Your girls certainly do know how to take matters into their own hands, Ms. Rapscott!"

The jogger and the policeman agreed heartily, though they couldn't say because their mouths were full of birthday cake.

A man with a saxophone was making his way across the room now, too. "Saxophone, Ms. Rapscott?"

The headmistress declined and excused herself politely to greet another guest. "Look, girls, it's the clerk from the birdseed store!" Ms. Rapscott made a little hop for joy.

A man with large round spectacles, red suspenders, and a polka-dotted bow tie came rushing toward her. "Took the pebble out of your shoe, I see, Ms. Rapscott." The clerk gave her a playful nudge with his elbow.

"You noticed!" Ms. Rapscott replied. "And I am having a *very* Good Day, thank you."

"How was that birdseed?" he asked.

"It could have been worse, thank you. Cake?" Ms. Rapscott offered him a piece just as two new guests arrived.

"Hello there!" It was the postman. Behind him was the Adventurer who strode purposefully into the class.

"I do love Great Rapscott Day!" he bellowed. He shook Ms. Rapscott's hand heartily while the corgis poured him his coffee and made up his dish of ice cream and cake.

There was one last guest.

"Happy Great Rapscott Day!" A young woman rode her bike right into the classroom. She was still in her wet suit and flippers.

"So glad you could make it," Ms. Rapscott said graciously. Lewis took her bike while Clark hurried to the refreshments table for her coffee and cake.

"You should have brought your dolphins," Ms. Rapscott said.

"Next time." The young woman smiled and leaned over to tell the headmistress, "I've just come back."

"Did you Go Far?" Ms. Rapscott asked.

"Did I!" She laughed, but then she grew serious and spoke in a low voice. "Were the girls disappointed that The Top was closed?"

"*So* disappointed," Ms. Rapscott replied.

"We got used to it, though." Bea was trying to push her way to where the cake was quickly disappearing. She got a plate and was about to take some cake when Lewis stopped her. Clark shook his head, took her plate and her fork, and set them back on the table.

"Not now, Bea!" Ms. Rapscott reprimanded her student. "Mingle with the guests! See if there is anything they need, class!" she ordered. "A Rapscott Girl is always a good hostess!"

The girls' mouths watered as their favorite birthday cake quickly disappeared without their being able to even have a morsel.

There was much chatter and laughter and clinking of forks on dishes and cups refilled.

Ms. Rapscott made sure that each of the girls spoke to every single person there and the talk swelled to a crescendo. The mayor, the Lady in Gold, the jogger, the woman and her parrot, the policeman, the saxophone player, the clerk, the postman, the adventurer, and the young woman in the wet suit all talked and ate ice cream and birthday cake until it was gone.

"Same time next year?" The mayor gave his mustache one last dab.

"Same time!" Ms. Rapscott said.

Then the guests all said what a great Great Rapscott Day it had been and left as quickly as they had come.

"They ate all the ice cream and cake," Bea said woefully.

"They always do," Ms. Rapscott said. "It's a tradition."

"But don't we get any?" Mildred asked.

"It's the one day of the year that we don't, class," Ms. Rapscott said. "That's a tradition as well."

The girls stared at the empty cake plate wondering what was so great about Great Rapscott Day.

No one said a word except for Mildred. "At least someone came."

Ms. Rapscott collected all the dishes and Lewis and Clark tidied up. "It's a tradition, girls. On Great Rapscott Day not a single parent has ever come to an Open House."

"Never?" Bea said.

"Never," Ms. Rapscott replied, and Bea felt a twinge of sadness. Mildred, Fay, Annabelle, and Dahlia did as well. All of the girls wished at the same time that they were like normal girls whose parents weren't so busy.

Chapter 23
GREAT RAPSCOTT TRADITIONS

*A*nd now it's time for the Great Medal Cere-mony, girls. Take a seat!"

Lewis stood next to Ms. Rapscott holding an opened briefcase where five gold medals were attached to blue and silver ribbons that shone richly against a black velvet interior. A diamond flashed from the etched drawing of a lighthouse on each medal. The girls strained forward in their seats to have a better look, and their hearts beat a little faster because they all wanted one for their own.

"How do you know when you've gone Far in Life?" Ms. Rapscott asked.

Bea was the first one with her hand raised. "When you've reached The Top!"

"Very good, Bea." Ms. Rapscott smiled broadly and made a little hop to show that she was pleased. "Congratulations, girls! All except one of you have failed the course!"

"Failed?" The color had drained from Bea's face. "We *failed*?"

The girls joined her and started talking all at once. "We failed, Ms. Rapscott? We really failed?"

"You cannot Go Far in Life unless you fail several times," Ms. Rapscott said merrily. "OH! I'm very, *very* proud of you, girls."

"But shouldn't I get a medal?" Fay called out. "I got to The Top!"

"You certainly did, Fay. Congratulations!" Ms. Rapscott exclaimed.

Clark placed the medal around Fay's neck and Lewis shook her hand.

"Ms. Rapscott! *Ms. Rapscott!*" Bea poked the air angrily with her raised hand. "But Fay never went to The Bottom or paid her dues or anything. She only got to The Top by mistake."

"Precisely, Bea," the headmistress said simply. "Which only proves that you *can* fail in the best possible way."

By now all the girls, except for Fay, were absolutely convinced that there was nothing at all that great about Great Rapscott Day.

"Now!" Ms. Rapscott clapped her hands together and there was a twinkle in her eye. "There's another great tradition we have on Great Rapscott Day and that is, once a year students get to visit the seventh floor. Come along, girls." Ms. Rapscott and Lewis and Clark disappeared up the spiral stairs.

Bea, Mildred, Annabelle, and Dahlia had all failed, and whether or not it was in the best possible way didn't seem to matter because they wouldn't be receiving the beautiful medal. They grumbled and muttered their discontent to one another the entire way up, past the kitchen, the bathroom, their dorm, Ms. Rapscott's room, and even the pajama room they'd loved going to last semester.

But when their heads poked through to the seventh floor they gasped.

There wasn't a giant spider in a cage, or a ghost, or a hair salon, or even a fabulous library like Annabelle had been so sure of. Instead, there was a life-sized oil painting of Amelia Earhart on one wall. Her scarf fluttered in a breeze. Her eyes sparkled back at the girls, following them wherever they went. On the opposite wall the school crest had been painted and every square inch of the walls was covered with a framed picture of a girl. There were hundreds and hundreds of pictures of girls their own age and of every sort that stared back at Bea, Mildred, Fay, Annabelle, and Dahlia.

Ms. Rapscott held out her arms and twirled around. "Welcome to the Great Rapscott Room! These are all my students, girls of busy parents just like you, who have come to Great Rapscott School to learn everything their parents were too busy to teach them."

The girls wandered spellbound around the room studying the pictures and looking at all the faces: ones who smiled brightly and ones that looked like they were on the verge of tears.

There were serious girls, studious girls, shy girls, laughing girls, dreamy-looking girls, girls of every color, size, and shape.

Ms. Rapscott went from one to the next telling a little about each. One was Known for Being a Complainer, but she had fallen arches which Ms. Rapscott said was a sure sign of someone who had good taste. Another was a dark-eyed girl who was Known for Always Interrupting People When They Talked, but she also had a bald spot on the left side of her head which meant she was lucky. There were girls known for all sorts of things: for being a know-it-all, for being a finicky eater, there was even one Known for Always Knocking Her Orange Juice Over Every Day at Breakfast.

In the faces of these girls Bea, Mildred, Fay, Annabelle, and Dahlia thought they saw a little bit of themselves. Bea stood before the picture of a sturdy girl with short, black choppy hair with a mole on the end of her nose in the shape of star.

Bea's mouth dropped open.

Ms. Rapscott was at Bea's side with her hands behind her back looking at the picture now, too. The headmistress tapped her chin with a finger and mused. "The Lady in Gold was just your age in that picture, Bea. As I recall she was a very bossy little girl Known for Always Having to Be First."

Bea looked down because it sounded a lot like herself.

Ms. Rapscott gave Bea a sidelong look. "But she was a born leader, that one!"

"She was?" Bea asked, amazed.

"Yes, Bea." Ms. Rapscott leaned over and whispered in her ear, "And so are you."

"I am?" Bea said incredulously.

Ms. Rapscott nodded crisply. "My girls have grown up to be all sorts of things," she explained. "One invented invisible crayons, another is a squirrel doctor, and another flies dirigibles."

Mildred looked at one girl who had red curly hair like hers. "What happened to her?"

"She is a very well-known translator," Ms. Rapscott said, pleased.

Mildred was puzzled. "What does she translate?"

"Dolphin," the headmistress replied, "and if anyone wants to know what one is saying this girl can tell them."

"But, Ms. Rapscott!" Mildred was excited because she suddenly realized that the woman who came to Great Rapscott Day wearing the wet suit had curly red hair and looked just like the girl in the picture. "Is the girl in the picture the same woman who was here today?"

"*All* the guests today were former students of mine and Mr. Everbest's!" Ms. Rapscott sang out. Then she went from picture to picture pointing them out. The jogger had grown up to make robots, the lady with the parrot made teapots, and at this time of the year she carved pumpkins to decorate the porches of everyone in town.

Annabelle pointed to the picture of a serious-looking girl with straight hair and thick glasses who looked a lot like her. "Did she ever learn to have FUN, Ms. Rapscott?"

"Indeed she did, Annabelle." Ms. Rapscott

made a little hop. "She grew up to build luxury tree houses for groundhogs."

Annabelle was puzzled. "But I didn't know that groundhogs liked to live in trees."

"No one knew—until my student came along." Ms. Rapscott looked very proud. "And now the groundhogs live in lovely light-filled houses. They hardly need to hibernate in the wintertime and have taken up tobogganing—can you imagine?"

Annabelle couldn't exactly imagine, but even to her it sort of sounded like a fun thing to do.

Ms. Rapscott continued. "The clerk from the birdseed store was always Known for Liking Polka Dots, but he was very fond of animals— especially birds," Ms. Rapscott said. "The mayor was Head Lad at Mt. Everbest for three consecutive years, and the adventurer had a sparkle in his eye just like you, Fay." Ms. Rapscott winked. Then she told the girls that all the children at both schools had become teachers, writers, scientists, astronauts, and astronomers. They were circus performers, singers, actors, and artists. "They were all very different but every one of them failed many times, and every one of them went far," Ms. Rapscott said proudly.

Dahlia looked at the picture of a little girl with big eyes and short yellow hair. "Who's she?"

"One of my favorite students, Dahlia!" Ms. Rapscott smiled. "She was very popular with the other girls, too, and she grew up and became a mother with a boy and a little girl of her own who she is never too busy to take care of."

"Is she happy?" Dahlia asked.

"She is *very* happy, Dahlia," Ms. Rapscott answered. "And now it's time for another tradition . . . the Great Rapscott School Ring Ceremony!"

On the wall there was a set of built-in drawers. Clark slid one open to reveal five gold rings with a stormy gray jewel that glittered in the center. The girls were stunned into silence, for none of them had ever seen or owned anything so beautiful.

The headmistress showed one to the girls. "You can see that the initials of the school are clearly engraved on each of your rings. While you are here you will always wear your ring so that the initials face outward to capture all the lessons and experiences that you will have in your years here at Great Rapscott School. Understood?"

The girls nodded with large serious eyes.

One by one Ms. Rapscott placed a ring on each girl's finger. Then she said, "Repeat after me: With this ring I will uphold the great tradition of Great Rapscott School and all Rapscott Girls the world over. I promise I will never be afraid to make mistakes, that I will take matters into my own hands, and that I will never let a disappointment keep me from going far."

Then the corgis appeared with cherry pie, which was also a tradition to eat on Great Rapscott Day. All the girls were happy now, even the ones who hadn't received a medal. They kept looking at their rings because the stone seemed to change color in the most mysterious way, and they talked and laughed.

Annabelle even realized that between the cherry pie, the beautiful ring, and all the excitement from the day's festivities she was enjoying herself immensely. She was, in fact, having something that she'd never had before. Annabelle had to tell someone. "Bea," she said in utter astonishment, "I think I'm having FUN."

"Are you sure?" Bea asked.

Annabelle thought about it and said, "Yes. I'm definitely having FUN."

"Me too." Bea grinned. All the others agreed that they were having FUN, too. Just as the girls were starting to agree that Great Rapscott Day really was great, Ms. Rapscott said, "It's time to leave, girls!"

Suddenly the room became quiet and one of them said in a low voice, "Leave the Great Rapscott Room?"

"Leave Great Rapscott!" Ms. Rapscott announced in a much chirpier tone than any of the girls thought she should have. "You must all go now!"

"But we don't want to leave." Bea groaned. "Not now, just when we're having so much FUN."

"And you said I didn't have to go home for a long, long time—y-you said I could stay right here—at school," Mildred cried. "That's exactly what you said, Ms. Rapscott!"

"Only if you didn't improve, Mildred," Ms. Rapscott said smoothly.

"But Ms. Rapscott—" Mildred wailed.

"Everyone is going—no one is staying!" the headmistress sang out.

"But our parents will lose us at the mall, Ms. Rapscott!" Dahlia said.

"And we'll get squashed in parking lots," Annabelle reminded her.

"Mine don't even know my name," Fay moaned.

"Your parents cannot help it, girls—they are busy," Ms. Rapscott said firmly. "Furthermore it's a tradition that all Rapscott Girls go home for a visit on Great Rapscott Day." She herded them out of the room and down the spiral stairs all the way to the classroom and outside where their boxes were waiting.

The girls burst into tears—even Annabelle— and none of them wanted to go. "Can't we stay?" she cried.

"Absolutely not!" Ms. Rapscott shaded her eyes and looked out to sea. "You must all go home to practice what you've learned this semester." Angry-looking clouds marched in from the north heralding Hurricane Dorothy who was on her way to Great Rapscott. "Be aware that you must be back on December ninth before midnight when winter starts.

"But winter starts on December twenty-first, it says so right in the *Encyclopedia Britannica*," Annabelle shouted.

"It may say so in the encyclopedia, Annabelle, but here in Big White Lighthouse by the Sea winter always arrives at midnight, December tenth, on the dot. You must be safely back at school before then. Any questions?"

The girls had so many questions that they didn't even know what to ask first.

"Your boxes will be ready for departure to bring you back to school on December ninth promptly at six a.m.," said the headmistress.

Since they'd been outside the sky had darkened with clouds, and a few raindrops plopped on their heads. The boxes were ready to be sealed, and Ms. Rapscott had some final words for the girls. "During the winter semester there will be many difficulties and problems to solve. The weather here will be at its absolute worst!" She made a little hop because there was nothing she loved better than a good blizzard. "You will be tested to see what you all are made of, girls, and it will be grueling." She beamed because there was nothing she found more thrilling than a grueling test to see what she was made of. There was a loud crack of thunder and it began to rain. "It's time, girls!"

"Good-bye, Mildred! Good-bye, Fay! Good-bye, Annabelle!" Bea called. Then even louder she shouted, "I'll miss you, Dahlia!" Bea had come to appreciate Dahlia's grit which is how it is when you have a lot of pluck.

Dahlia found herself shouting back, "I'll miss you too, Bea!" After all the two girls had been through, Dahlia had come to appreciate Bea's pluck, which is how it is when you have a lot of grit.

"Do you have Harold?" Fay asked Dahlia, and was relieved to see that she did. "Good-bye!"

"Good-bye, Dahlia!" Mildred called.

"Good-bye, Mildred!" Dahlia called back to the red-haired girl who was still her best friend at Great Rapscott School.

The corgis pealed off the kwik-close tape on the E-Z shut flaps and sealed the boxes all except one.

"Ms. Rapscott! Ms. Rapscott!" Annabelle shouted, and she waved her hand and would not allow the corgi to seal hers. "Just so you know—*I* know these boxes fly."

They stared at each other but Annabelle of course blinked first because no one could ever win a staring contest with Ms. Rapscott. The sky suddenly was black as night and the clouds opened up. The rain forced the girl to take cover inside her box, and it was sealed.

There was a fierce gust of wind, and Annabelle could feel the box bump along the ground. She burrowed herself in the packing material, but she couldn't help feeling excited. She had come to love this part of the trip. She hugged herself and closed her eyes when the box took off, and even though she had just learned how, she knew for sure that she was having FUN.

Bea settled into the packing material to make herself comfortable. She hadn't been Head Girl this semester like she'd hoped . . . or made it to The Top like Fay, but Bea couldn't help feeling happy. She thought about what Ms. Rapscott had told her in the Great Rapscott Room and decided maybe it wasn't so important to be first all the time after all. The box rose and tipped to this side and that as it whirled around the lighthouse. She checked to make sure her snacks were close by because there was nothing like a good cracker and some cheese when you're flying through the air in a box. Bea closed her eyes and whispered, *I'm a born leader.*

As soon as Mildred's box was sealed her light clicked on. She dried her eyes and took out her notebook to write. "Hi, it's me, Mildred A'Lamode from Great Rapscott School." Mildred stopped to make sure that there were enough crackers and cheese. There were. But what should she write? Images flickered across her mind of where she'd been and all she'd done. Mildred suddenly felt a swell of pride in herself and began to write: "I used to be afraid to leave my room . . ." She stopped and saw herself riding in the mayor's barrel across a stormy sea, she was hanging off the end of a bunch of balloons, her legs dangling, her slippers skimming the tops of trees in the night sky, and there she was hiking up the road that would take her straight to The Top. She wrote: "But now I'm not afraid anymore because this semester I went far."

Inside Fay's box the sparkle in her eye was every bit as bright as the diamond on her gold Great Rapscott Medal for Reaching The Top. She could do little more than gaze at it and grin. She would never take it off, and the next time that she did something wrong Fay knew all she had to do was touch her medal to remind herself that it really was possible to make mistakes in the best possible way. She could feel the box climbing upward and Fay sighed. They'd all be back in a month just before winter. Fay tried to imagine the snowy adventures Ms. Rapscott had in store for them, and she shivered with anticipation. She had hardly left but she couldn't wait to get back.

Dahlia Thistle sat in the corner of her box and could feel the wind lifting it upward. She was so small that Lewis and Clark had stuffed it with extra packing to keep her from being tossed about. Being in the box had made her nervous ever since she'd tumbled out of it last semester . . . but not anymore. "Don't be afraid, Harold, I'm here," she said with all the authority of a true Rapscott Head Girl. She patted her pocket where Harold sat snug, and then suddenly she noticed a strange glimmer of light that danced around inside the box. It took her a few moments before she realized it was coming from her school ring! And when she looked it glittered so oddly that she stared at it to make sure that what she was seeing was not some trick of her imagination.

Deep inside the ring a lighthouse appeared, tiny enough for a creature no bigger than the dot over an "i." She looked closer still to see Ms. Rapscott and Lewis and Clark, who stood on the lookout tower and waved. Dahlia waved back, delighted but completely unsurprised. By now she knew anything was possible when it came to Ms. Rapscott.

The wind blew fiercely and the rain came down in torrents beating the lighthouse. But it wasn't until Bea, Mildred, Fay, Annabelle, and Dahlia had disappeared from sight over the horizon that the headmistress and her faithful corgis went inside and bolted the door against the angry weather.

They went down the spiral stairs to their cozy room that was like the inside of a ship's cabin.

"So there it is," Ms. Rapscott said sadly. "They're gone, boys."

The corgis sighed and their shoulders slumped.

"But never fear!" she added. "The girls will be back right before the first blizzard."

Lewis took off his watch and Clark put away his clipboard. Ms. Rapscott kicked off her boots and poured the hot chocolate. "To the winter semester. May it be full of blizzards with zero visibility, whiteout conditions, and drifts all the way up to the top of the lighthouse!"

The three clinked their mugs together. Ms. Rapscott sat in her chair by the woodstove and Clark brought her the Great Rapscott Lesson Book.

"Which one, boys?" she asked.

Clark pointed at a page and Lewis's eyes lit up.

"How to Be Ready for Anything," Ms. Rapscott said. "One of my favorites!"

The corgis grinned because it was one of theirs as well.

She pulled from her pocket a tattered, worn map of the island. Rain lashed the lighthouse and the wind battered the windows.

"Isn't it thrilling!" she exclaimed.

Then all three settled down to decide which snowy places would be the best to visit so that they could be ready for anything when the girls returned.

Ms. Rapscott and the girls had
their first grand adventure in

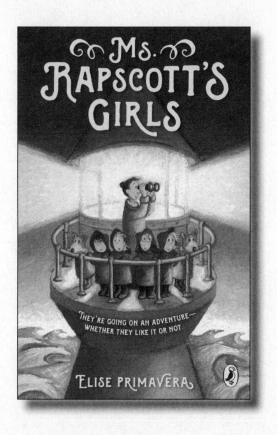

Turn the page for a preview!

Chapter 1

BEATRICE

It was a perfect day for getting Lost on Purpose.

Ms. Rapscott stood at dawn on the observation deck of the lighthouse that was Great Rapscott School for Girls of Busy Parents. A huge beam of light rotated slowly above her. The teacher peered through binoculars while her two corgis looked on.

Armies of dark clouds marched ominously in from the west. The weather would be bad—but here in Big White Lighthouse by the Sea the weather was always bad. "Do you think it will storm, boys?"

Lewis licked the tip of a paw and held it up in the air to check the direction of the wind. Clark nodded a confirmation; it *would* most likely storm.

Ms. Rapscott scanned the horizon and, in the distance, she saw five faint objects whizzing through the air. They were in a V formation—a pattern used by geese flying south for the winter. But these were not geese, these were boxes—five large boxes. They flew north over the sea road that snaked along the cliff of the rocky coast, straight for the school. "They're here!" She hurried inside, and clattered around and around, down the circular staircase. Lewis remembered his watch and hurried to strap it on his wrist, and Clark grabbed his clipboard with the list of names. Then they both followed a moment behind.

Thump!

Thump!

Thump!

Thump!

Thump!

The boxes landed on the front porch of Great Rapscott School for Girls of Busy Parents.

The teacher poked the first box with her foot.

"Let me out!" came a voice from inside the box.

"Stand back!" Ms. Rapscott warned.

The dogs kept a safe distance.

The headmistress pulled the E-Z open tab with one quick zip and leaped away. A second later, out popped a girl.

"Where am I!?" she hollered.

"You are at Great Rapscott School," Ms. Rapscott replied. "What is your name?"

"Beatrice Chissel!!" Beatrice had been packed wearing a soiled plaid jumper and shirt, the uniform from a previous school that she had been kicked out of some weeks ago. Her short dark hair looked as if she'd cut it herself, her nose was running, and her teeth needed brushing. She didn't smell very good, either.

Lewis checked his watch; it was 7:00 a.m. sharp. Clark put a checkmark next to her name.

"This one's got pluck!" Ms. Rapscott winked at her corgis.

Beatrice Chissel was very small and round, like a beach ball with arms and legs. She narrowed her eyes and gave Ms. Rapscott a suspicious look, then bounced off the porch to take it all in.

She lifted her snub nose and sniffed the salt sea air. She cocked an ear and listened to the racket made by the waves that crashed against large pointy rocks. She felt the sand sting her podgy cheeks like little needles. A clamshell bopped her on the head from a passing seagull and that was it.

Beatrice Chissel climbed back inside her box and pulled the flaps over her head. "Mail me back!!" For once her shrill voice was muffled, which was highly unusual because, for such a young girl, she had developed a set of lungs the size and strength of a professional hog caller.

The reason for this was that no one ever heard Beatrice unless she screamed.

Her parents, Dr. Loulou Chissel and Dr. Lou Chissel, were very busy. They had started out in the cinder-block business and slowly but surely had worked their way up to become prominent cosmetic surgeons. In a stroke of genius Beatrice's father, Dr. Lou Chissel, had even devised a way to fill out wrinkles and lips from the raw materials that he had used to make his cinder blocks.

"It's a win-win situation," Dr. Lou often said.

But the Chissels didn't stop there. Dr. Loulou Chissel had shortened her daughter's name from Beatrice to Bea to save time, because Dr. Chissel was busy experimenting with ways to grow hair on cinder blocks.

"Just think of the possibilities," she crowed.

Dr. Lou rubbed his bald head, "Just think."

As you can imagine, all this thinking required a great deal of quiet. But their daughter, Bea, was always wanting something—like breakfast—and she was always asking questions like, "What's a birthday present?"

When no one answered she would get louder and louder, until she would shriek at a decibel loud enough to shatter glass:

"What's a birthday present?!!!!!!"

This is how Beatrice Chissel became Known for Being Loud.

To keep her quiet Bea's parents made her count cinder blocks, and enter the number in a spiral notebook labeled: NUMBER OF CINDER BLOCKS. So far she had counted 637,523 cinder blocks.

Now she was at Great Rapscott School, and she would not be mailed back home. Instead, in only a matter of hours, Beatrice Chissel would be utterly Lost on Purpose.

Chapter 2

MILDRED, FAY, ANNABELLE, AND DAHLIA

There was a distinct snoring sound coming from the second box.

ZI-I-I-I-I-IP! Ms. Rapscott pulled the E-Z open tab. Sure enough, inside the box Lewis found a student curled up fast asleep. Ms. Rapscott nudged her and leaned over to look inside. "What is your name?"

"Mildred A'Lamode," she said with a mighty yawn.

"OH! This one is *perfect*. Look at her hair!" Ms. Rapscott had a theory that girls with curly red hair were always loaded with enthusiasm.

Mildred had on her favorite pink pajamas with the yellow ducks on them. They were two sizes too small because she'd been wearing them since she was six.

Of course her mother and father were too busy to get her new ones. Mimi and Marcel A'Lamode were a song-and-dance team, as well as internationally acclaimed chefs who were famous for a dish called *les grenouilles et escargots,* which was basically frogs' legs with snails. They had a huge following on their popular TV show where they whipped up French recipes while performing popular French songs like *Frère Jacques.*

Mildred was excited to learn all she could from her parents, but she always got in the way.

"Mon Dieu!" her mother exclaimed when Mildred asked for the thousandth time how to make a cake in the shape of the Eiffel Tower.

"Sacre Bleu!" her father declared. His soufflé was sinking and his flambé was fizzling; he couldn't stop to teach his daughter the lyrics to *Alouette*!

Mimi and Marcel A'Lamode didn't even have

time to show Mildred how to stuff an éclair—
they had a lot to do.

Mildred on the other hand had nothing to do,
but eventually she did find a hobby . . . something
she liked and that she was good at. She watched
TV, in her pink pajamas with the yellow ducks
on them. She also got to see her parents as much
as she wanted—on TV.

This is how Mildred A'Lamode became Known
for Being Lazy.

Mildred woke up and stretched. She poked
her head out of the box and remembered that she
didn't like being outside. The world felt so big,
and it made her uneasy. She peeked over the rim
and wondered what kind of a place she had landed
in where it was normal for a dog to be able to
check your name off a list. Mildred wished she
was back home in her room—even if she had to
eat frogs' legs for the rest of her life.

Ms. Rapscott moved to the third box.

The flaps opened and quick as can be the girl
inside tried to hop out, but she caught a toe and
fell flat on her face onto the porch.

"What is your name?" The teacher asked as she had the others.

"I'm May Fandrake—I mean I'm Day Frandake—I mean I'm *Fay* Mandrake!"

Fay Mandrake had buckteeth, a small pink nose, and light blond hair, which gave her a sort of rabbity look.

"This one's got a sparkle in her eye." Ms. Rapscott thought that a sparkle in the eye was the sign of an adventurous spirit.

Clark checked her name off the list.

Fay wore a long ragged T-shirt and tights that wouldn't stay up because she had put them on backward.

Her parents were famous for having two sets of octuplets. They were very busy. To keep track of all the babies, they named the first bunch "L" names and the second bunch "N" names. Fay always wanted to help, but she would dress Larry and Lee in pink T-shirts while Laura and Lily would be dressed in blue. She was constantly mixing up Nancy with Noelle, and Nicholas with

Nate. Finally the only thing she was allowed to do was mop the floors.

This is how Fay became Known for Not Being Able to Do Anything Right. Her nose twitched and her eyes darted about nervously. She yanked at her tights and was relieved when everyone's attention shifted to the fourth box.

Lewis waited there for Ms. Rapscott to open it. She pulled the E-Z open tab and a girl with horn-rimmed glasses and long, straight black hair to her waist stepped out. Without having to be asked or offering even a suggestion of a smile she said, "My name is Annabelle Merriweather."

Annabelle wore a pair of running shoes that were five sizes too big and a peanut-butter-and-jelly-stained T-shirt that had been given away free at some sporting event. The shirt hung well below her knees and had a slogan on the front with a smiley face that said: BECAUSE YOU'RE WORTH IT.

"This one is *very* bright," Ms. Rapscott said with authority. "I'll bet you've read the entire *Encyclopedia Britannica*."

Annabelle nodded. She had read the entire *Encyclopedia Britannica* but only because there was nothing else to do. Her mother and father were very busy—they were professional exercisers.

"Your father and I are going out for a run now, dear," Annabelle's mother would say.

"But you just came *in* from a run," Annabelle would complain.

As professional exercisers it was not unusual for the Merriweathers to go out in the morning for a run and not come back for a couple of weeks. Of course they always made sure that their daughter had plenty of peanut butter and jelly to hold her until they returned, but needless to say it wasn't a great arrangement. The Merriweathers were lucky, though, that Annabelle could take care of herself, which is how she became Known for Being Old for Her Age.

Annabelle looked with distaste at the other girls and exhaled loudly through her teeth—a mannerism which she had no doubt picked up from some adult.

There was only one more name on the student

list. Clark stood ready to check "Dahlia Thistle" off. Lewis watched while Ms. Rapscott set to opening the fifth box.

"Oh, dear!" Ms. Rapscott said as she realized there would be no need to open the fifth box. Someone had failed to pull off the kwik-close tape to secure the E-Z shut flaps.

Lewis shook his head sadly, and so did Clark.

"Her mother forgot," Ms. Rapscott sighed. "Probably because she was so busy."

Of all the girls, Dahlia Thistle's family had the distinction of being the busiest. Dahlia's mother wrote a very popular blog about the trials and tribulations of being a mom. This took a lot of her time, but it was difficult because Dahlia was always crying over something like a bad dream, and always badgering her mother to read her a bedtime story.

So Dahlia's mother gave her to her father who was a professional comment writer. He wrote comments on the Internet about toothpaste, shoelaces, shaving cream, dishwashing detergent, bug spray, slipcovers, you name it.